To Margaret,
With Best Wishes,
Tamar 5.12.22

GLADWELL THE PARODIST

a whydunnit

Tamar Yellin

Gladwell the Parodist
Copyright © 2022 by Tamar Yellin

This edition copyright © 2022 Cadmus Press. All rights reserved. No part of this publication may be reproduced in whole or in part, or stored in a retrieval system, or transmitted in any form or by any means, electronic, mechanical, photocopying, recording, or otherwise, without written permission from the publisher.

ISBN: 978-4-908793-56-1

Cover: Tamar Yellin

Cadmus Press
cadmusmedia.org

GLADWELL THE PARODIST

a whydunnit

Tamar Yellin

Cadmus Press
2022

— I —

EVERYONE WANTS TO KNOW who killed Gladwell the Parodist. Broadsheets to tabloids, the papers are full of it. Yet until the discovery of his murdered corpse, media interest in him was muted, to say the least. Who cares about writers, unless they are rich and famous? Even the juiciest literary scandals rarely make it beyond the cultural pages. The career of a bit-player, a satirist whose work was known only to aficionados, was hardly headline material. His murder changed all that. The moment his body was found he became a celebrity, not, it is true, of the kind he aspired to be in life, but a celebrity nevertheless. Of course, Gladwell himself is not around to enjoy his hour in the sun. One can only hope he would have taken some bitter pleasure in the irony of it.

Everybody wants to know whodunnit. And as rapidly became apparent, there are numerous candidates. Rarely, perhaps, has there been a writer whom so many other writers wanted dead, not that they would ever admit it, of course. To do so would be to confess that his parodies had teeth. Whereas the gracious way to deal with a parody of oneself is to laugh it off, make light of it, be a good sport; even, if one is of a self-deprecating turn, to say that it is spot-on. And yet there must be so many victims of Ralph Gladwell who have ground their teeth in the knowledge that no-one, reading his parodies of their work, would ever be able to take them entirely seriously again. There must be so many—too many to count—who have wanted, at least for a moment, to drive the point of a nib into his heart.

It's the business of the press to speculate, and the papers have done so with gusto, by publishing the most pungent snippets from Gladwell's cruellest travesties of our most august figures: Nobel laureates, Booker prize-winners, Orange and Costa and Impac grandees, not to mention those who may not have been recipients of any of these awards, but soar above them in the splendour of their reputation. The unspoken question to the public is: What would you do in their place? The invited answer: Take out a contract on the little shit. What a feast for journalists if we could only get a Pulitzer winner in the dock!

Such a dramatic outcome can't be discounted, of course. But the killing of Ralph Gladwell is far more likely to be the work of some lesser mortal, a young debut author still wearing his nervous system on the outside, some sensitive soul for whom his merciless ridicule proved too much. A worthy woman novelist, perhaps, watching the dismemberment of her ninth heartfelt and overrated book, or a self-important politico with a God-given right to be taken seriously. The despair, frustration, even murderous rage felt by such people could certainly drive them to a desperate act, and should never be underestimated.

Meanwhile, the police have been conducting their own more scientific investigations. The victim was found slumped over his desk at his house in Tufnell Park. Suicide could be ruled out, unless he had somehow managed to stab himself in the back several times with what seems to have been rather a blunt knife. Apparently one of the wild thrusts pierced his heart, and his subsequent death must have been almost instantaneous. The house had been ransacked, but what, if anything, had been taken remains a mystery.

The corpse of an approximately fifty-year-old male, six foot four, thin to the point of emaciation, with aquiline features and a rockstar ponytail: it could hardly have been anyone but he. Identification of the body was made additionally certain, as everyone knows, by the gold jewellery found upon it: the identity bracelet with the inscription "C.3.3" and the engraved wedding ring from Aaron Milner. These objects have exerted a poignant influence over those writing and reading about the case, with their suggestion of uncharacteristic sentimentality in one so cynical.

All of a sudden the hidden life of a writer acknowledged as brilliant by many, if in a limited and somehow disappointing way, has become a source of fascination to high- and lowbrow alike. Given the gruesome nature of the murder, the possible celebrity of the murderer and their ample motive—not to mention the colourful character of the victim—this is a story that could run and run. And yet the life of Ralph Gladwell remains, for the most part, shrouded in mystery.

That is where I come in.

— II —

I have been interested in Gladwell for a long time. I first began reading his blog a good five years ago, in fact I would say I was among its earliest followers. I loved his work. His wit was irresistible. He made me laugh.

His parodies might be in prose or poetry, of authors alive or dead, household names or merely fashionable. Of course, they were never entirely obscure, for what would be the point of parodying an author hardly anyone has ever read? In this, you might say, there is a natural justice, sparing the failed writer the pain of further ridicule, while the successful one pays their dues through ritual humiliation. Parody, in fact, might be considered the revenge of the failed writer upon the fêted.

For those of us enjoying Gladwell's blog, these matters were of lively interest, if the entries in the commentary box were anything to go by. When Twitter started up we carried on the argument there, and a large community established itself on Facebook. The assumption by most of us was that "Gladwell" was a pseudonym, combining as it did an expression of how he felt and how he did. Online aliases were, after all, the norm, "Maximum Beerbohm," for instance, or "skewered-n-wriggling," but these acolytes, clever as they may be, were no match for the man himself. There was something just too *generous* about them.

When I say generous I do not mean that they were kindly or giving towards the Parodist's victims. On the contrary, it was their expressions of contempt that were over-generous, their readiness to eviscerate and condemn. Their abundance of bitterness, you might say, by which they merely exposed their own vulnerability and gave themselves away. These were very disappointed people. Gladwell never did that. His parodies were brilliant; his comments always keen and to the point. And he was good-natured.

I enjoyed the discussions, but rarely made a comment of my own. I have never been one to expose myself, and still find the public discourse on the internet altogether brutal and intimidating. That is part of its fascination, of course. Call me a coward, but I prefer to sit on the sidelines and observe. That, to me, has always been one of the essentials of being a writer.

Anyway, as I said, I pride myself on having been among the first followers. Gradually, over the years, Gladwell the Parodist acquired a large audience, until the blog started to be mentioned in the same breath as *The Onion* and *Private Eye*. Eventually it became something of a gauge of literary success to have been parodied by him, a sign of irrelevance to be overlooked. Not that such a mark of favour wasn't a two-edged sword, reputations being simultaneously recognised and demolished by it. Yet, as Gladwell often pointed out, the truly great writer is arguably unparodiable, nor can their work be seriously harmed by the parodist. Gladwell never attempted Shakespeare, for instance.

All this time I was at work on my own first novel, and it was through observation of Gladwell's razor surgery—here dismantling a writer's clunky plot, there exaggerating their awful style, elsewhere exposing their tedious obsessions—that I strove to avoid falling into the same errors. It made hard work of things. I started over more times than I can count. I would write a chapter, feel pleased with it, then read it (as I imagined) through Gladwell's eyes, and it would be reduced to no more than a list of potential howlers. My style was pretentious, my dialogue risible, my characters absurd. In setting myself the goal of writing something Gladwell would be unable to parody I merely succeeded in tying myself in knots.

But I kept trying. Since childhood I had dreamed of being a writer. I even felt it my destiny to be a great one. My ambition was to complete a novel that I would send to Gladwell, only to receive his flabbergasted response: I cannot parody this. It is sublime. It is untouchable. It is beyond parody. Gladwell's was the one seat of judgment from which I sought approval. All other critics were vain, mediocre, sentimental or quite simply stupid. Their opinions did not count. Gladwell had often parodied them.

In all this I never attempted the obvious: to write humorously. Everything I wrote was deeply serious, in fact, I was of the snobbish opinion that humour and greatness were incompatible. I failed to realise that to be a genuinely funny writer is just as difficult as to be a great one.

In any case, I never finished my novel and I never sent it to Gladwell for his opinion. The task I had set myself was simply impossible. Little by little, I was worn down. As I passed thirty—milestone and tombstone—my callow belief in myself crumbled, my dreams died. When I did approach him directly, it was with quite different material, and long after I had abandoned all hope of becoming a novelist.

— III —

THE FUNERAL TOOK PLACE a month after the discovery of the body, when the police and forensics team finally released it for burial. It was brought back to Gladwell's home town of High Wycombe, where his mother still lived on a genteel housing estate. A lot of his London friends were deeply surprised by these mundane provincial origins. Ralph had always given the impression that he was upper class, from some decayed aristocratic family perhaps, with his eccentric waistcoats, long hair and aquiline features. The truth, as I was to discover, was rather different.

A good many people came down for the service, High Wycombe not being quite distant or provincial enough to put them off. If it had been Nottingham or Dewsbury, for example, I doubt whether most of them would have bothered. Ralph had a core of friends who loved and indeed venerated him—I will come to them later—and a lot of hangers-on who liked to party. Then there were the literary people: those of them who had not been personally wounded by the Parodist's wit, or who adored him for having made fun of their rivals, or who had laughed at themselves along with him and forgiven him. But most of Gladwell's friends were non-literary types. He spent much of his time with artists, actors and musicians, and, naturally, a constant stream of dancers, models, waiters, construction workers and despatch-riders, all of whom were beautiful young men. Everywhere you looked in church that day (Ralph surprised us again by his expressed wish for a religious service) there were angels.

Of course, the press were there too, and what they were hoping for—what we were all hoping for, I imagine—was a glimpse of Aaron, but Aaron did not show. Someone said he was in the Mediterranean on his father's yacht, someone else that he was holed up in his Knightsbridge flat, hiding from reporters. The police had interviewed him, but he hadn't spoken a single word to the newspapers. We could only speculate as to whether he was grieving.

Ralph's mother Eileen and a couple of elderly men who, from their hawklike profiles, one assumed to be his uncles, sat in the front pew near the coffin. I knew that Ralph's father had died when he was twelve; it was one of the few personal details he had ever confided. Understandably, his mother was distraught. She was a tall slim woman who bore no further resemblance to her only son, apart from an uncannily familiar keenness of eye which, when it first met mine, made the hairs rise on the back of my neck. These three, along with a few other people, accompanied the coffin to the crematorium, after which we were all invited to join them for the wake at a hotel on the edge of town.

I don't think they had expected quite so many people to turn up. The buffet was scanty, but there was a bar, so the mourners did what came naturally and proceeded to get drunk. I thought Eileen and her brothers-in-law were pretty game. They seemed conventional types, and must have been slightly alarmed at the pierced and tattooed youngsters who had piled in from London, but they talked politely with everyone and thanked them for coming. I thought Eileen—Mrs Gladwell—had a certain grace, and that she must once have been a beautiful young woman. She intimidated me a little, given the programme of subterfuge I had in mind. But I screwed up my courage and approached her.

"Lovely service," I said as we shook hands, though there had been very little about it that was non-generic, only the briefest eulogy, nothing to reveal much about Ralph as a person; perhaps the very reason he had requested a religious funeral. "I'm very sorry for your loss."

"Thank you. Thank you for coming, Mr—?"

"Tate. Jim Tate. It's a privilege to meet Ralph's mother at last."

She smiled down on me. "Well, I'm very glad to meet you too. Did you know Ralph long?"

"It depends how you mean. I knew him a lot longer online than I did in person." I could tell this was mildly puzzling to her, so I went on, "I knew him best in the last two or three years. We worked together."

"At the university?"

"What? Oh, no—I mean his other work."

She looked blank for a moment. "Oh—you mean his writing. I always thought of that as more of a hobby. Then you're a writer also, Mr—?"

"Tate. Well, a writer of sorts. In fact, I was wondering—" she was already turning away; there were too many other calls on her attention—"I was wondering if I might ask for your help. You see, I've been thinking of writing a book about your son."

That was when she fixed me in her eagle gaze. I shuddered and beneath my plausible demeanour, felt a clutch of anxiety. "A book? About Ralph?"

"Yes."

"You mean a biography?"

"Perhaps not a conventional biography. More of a study."

"Of his—work?"

"His work, yes, but in relation to his personality. You see, I'm very interested in the nature of parody. In what goes toward the making of a great parodist."

Her left eye twitched slightly. I could tell she was torn: drawn to my proposal and at the same time sceptical.

"I feel sure that an understanding of his early life would be essential to such an analysis," I added.

"Yes," she replied thoughtfully, "yes, you're probably right." Then her eye locked in again. "So—it would be purely a literary study? It wouldn't have anything to do with … the way he died?"

"Oh, no, no! Nothing to do with that!"

I believe my shocked response must have done the trick, because she broke once more into a smile. "In that case, I'll be pleased to help you, as far as I can."

"Thank you. Thank you very much indeed."

We arranged to meet the following week, and congratulating myself on a fine performance I returned to the bar. I'd been there not more than two or three minutes when one of the beautiful young men came up beside me and ordered a pint of bitter shandy. It wasn't an accident, his standing there, because while he was waiting for his drink he turned to me and said, "I've seen you somewhere before, but I can't place you."

I remained as I was, hunched over the bar. "Well, we all knew Ralph," I said.

"Did you use to come to the Welly?"

"Hardly."

"Oh," he said. His drink arrived and he paid for it. "Well, fuck you, then."

"Not me, you won't," I replied softly as he departed. I finished up my orange juice and left soon after.

— IV —

I'd been following Gladwell's blog for two or three years before I finally plucked up the courage to get in touch. His email address was freely available, but I'd heard on the grapevine that he only occasionally replied to private messages, and generally out of sexual rather than literary motives. I had no interest in seeking to seduce him sexually, but it was my most urgent aspiration to do so intellectually. I sent him a parody. It was the first I had ever written, and I'd been perfecting it for six weeks.

I hardly dared hope I'd receive any reply, and was shocked at the way my heart pounded when I saw his tag in my inbox only a day later. For several minutes I hadn't the nerve to click on it, pretending to myself to be busy with other things. I feared the brush-off, something cutting from which I wouldn't easily recover, a pithy phrase of dismissal which would ring in my mind for ever. I was only half-disappointed, when I opened it up at last, to find a single line:

> *The piece isn't bad, but isn't DHL a rather easy target?*
> *G*

A range of emotions coursed through me, from relief to pleasure to frustration to indignation. Gladwell himself, after all, had written a parody of D. H. Lawrence four or five years back; I could readily locate it in his archive. I suppose I hadn't thought it one of his better jags, and believed myself capable of improving on it. The thought struck me, like a lightning flash, that Gladwell was jealous. He remembered his own attempt, and knew that mine was better. His only recourse was to diss the whole enterprise.

My first impulse was to fire off a reply, barbed and sarcastic, by which I would show that I had him rumbled. The piquant sentences were already racing through my head. But my hand hesitated above the keyboard. I am, as I think I have hinted, a cautious person. Think twice is my motto, and on second thoughts it became clear to me that there were several disadvantages to putting Gladwell's back up. First of all, by doing so I would only make it apparent that he had put up mine. Then, it was hardly in my interest to kill off a nascent friendship—or, if that was going too far, an association—that I had long desired, before it had even got past the opening stages. I certainly didn't want to suck up to Gladwell—that wouldn't impress him—but I didn't want to alienate him either. I thought long and deeply before making my response, longer and more deeply, perhaps, over this one sentence, than I had over many a paragraph of my precious novel.

Whom would you consider a hard target?

The reply came back within a couple of hours:

K.M.
G

Who the hell did he mean? Then it occurred to me: if we were sticking with D. H. Lawrence, early twentieth century, Bloomsbury et al (Lawrence was not strictly speaking Bloomsbury, but he'd passed their way) then he must be referring to that other satellite of the Bloomsbury set, Lawrence's fellow consumptive, Katherine Mansfield.

I had hardly read any Katherine Mansfield. Only a rather soppy story of hers we had covered in school what felt like centuries ago, about a garden party. Was Gladwell winding me up? He was quite capable of it. Get me to inhabit the prissy mind of a precious Edwardian lady, don her stays and bustle, promenade in the park and drink afternoon tea. That would teach me to tackle red-blooded David Herbert.

Then it struck me that I was thinking entirely my way, not Gladwell's. And what's more, I wasn't thinking like a parodist. Firstly, if Mansfield was all lace petticoats and china teacups, then I could make fun of that; moreover, if Gladwell considered her a hard target, then he must admire her on the literary level. I realised I had some serious reading to do.

I pulled her complete stories off the internet and set to work. And quickly I saw that she was indeed going to be difficult, harder at least than Lawrence; but there is nothing a parodist likes more than a challenge. Her early stories were flashy and efficient, and betrayed a rather cheap cynicism, I thought. Her later ones were subtle, with a glimmering quality not easily grasped. They were like Impressionist paintings. They had their fair share of teacups and even walks in the park, but these were somehow compromised, their seeming integrity ready to fly apart.

I did my research, as a parodist must. I read about

her short, disease-scarred life. I examined her portrait, with its sharp hard nose and chin and faraway gaze, and skimmed through her letters and diaries. I got down to taking notes on her vulnerabilities. She could be a bitch to her friends, and the marriage to Middleton Murray was a farce. As for her writing, there was danger in her very deliciousness; one could exaggerate that. Those fey little exclamations got on one's nerves. Let's face it, she frequently verged on the whimsical. And yet—here was the killer, this was where I could really twist the knife—that streak of nastiness, that sharp-chinned cynicism, was still there like the pattern in a stick of rock. That, together with too much poignancy, left a strange taste in the mouth. I thought I had her number.

So often, parody is regarded as simple caricature, the stretching of a long nose here, the startling of a wide eye there, an ugly face made grotesque, a beautiful one vulgar. There is a certain truth in that, but in fine parody there is more to it. The talented parodist gets his scalpel under the skin, dissects the subject, exposes them without mercy. He has an understanding of human nature.

It took me a good three weeks to perfect my parody of Katherine Mansfield. There was a crystalline focus to her sentences in which it was not easy to find the flaw. How do you make fun of prose in which every word is exactly right, each image freshly accurate? It was necessary to paint with a broader brush, distort the characters, who were too Renoir, crank up the dialogue, which could be precious, ridicule the situations, which trembled on the edge of portentousness. And make hay with those little puffball exclamations. Oh!

When I had finally finished, I read it aloud to myself and felt poisonously well pleased. Then I sent it off to Gladwell. And waited.

— V —

On a fine sunny afternoon in mid-July I approached Mrs Gladwell's neat suburban house and rang the bell. While waiting for it to be answered I stepped back a couple of paces and looked up at the building Ralph Gladwell had, between the ages of eleven and eighteen, improbably called home.

It stood on one of those well-heeled estates where each house is slightly different, but not different enough to have true individuality. In this they were supposed, no doubt, to reflect the people who lived in them: white-collar cogs in the machine of society. One had a cherry tree in the garden, another a weeping willow; the Gladwell house had a magnolia, large and venerable enough to have been there when Ralph was a boy, and a well-tended border of bright yellow roses. The house itself presented a large gable to the front, and big windows with leaded panes; to the side was a lesser gable with a smaller window. I peered up at this, wondering greedily whether it belonged to Ralph's teenage bedroom.

Eileen Gladwell opened the front door, elegant in navy-blue slacks and a floral blouse. "Mr Tate," she said, and I answered, "Please call me Jim." "Jim," she said. "Do come in. How was your journey?" "Fine, absolutely fine." "You found the house all right?" "No problem at all." Her greeting was slightly nervous, she gave me a cold English smile; and she stepped aside and ushered me indoors.

The hall was rigidly tidy, and smelt of air freshener. There was a bouquet of fake flowers in a vase on the windowsill and a framed painting of a Parisian café on the wall, the kind of thing tourists buy on holiday. The house was quiet, still, scrubbed and polished to within an inch of its life, and I felt a sense of suffocation which was deepened rather than alleviated as we walked through into the immaculate lounge with its patterned carpet and draylon-covered suite.

"Please make yourself at home," Mrs Gladwell said, indicating an armchair. "Would you like some tea?"

"Thank you," I replied, but didn't sit down. I had noticed an array of framed photographs on the mantelpiece, and couldn't resist going over to examine them. "Is this Ralph?"

"Yes. When he was seven." She joined me by the fireplace. "And this was taken when he was twenty-one." She picked up the latter portrait and, after contemplating it for a few moments, handed it to me. I saw a young man with long dark hair and a paisley scarf wrapped foppishly around his neck. It was recognisably the Parodist, but with a face so callow, so unformed, that I had to suppress a smile. The high-bridged nose, which had always made him appear haughty and eccentric, emerged from smooth and strangely alien terrain. But the sharp eye was there, gazing out at me with its gimlet intelligence, so that on replacing the picture I felt a strong impulse to turn it to the wall.

"And this is Ralph's father, I suppose."

"Yes, that's Barry." Her eye fell fondly on the picture of a tense-looking man with his tie fastened too tight, seventies sideburns and the same aquiline profile as his son. He and the two uncles who had appeared at the funeral might have been triplets.

"He was only forty-seven when he died. Thank heaven he took out decent life insurance." She added, "The photos keep me company."

"Of course." I looked again at the seven-year-old Gladwell, who had a child's button nose and fair hair, but whose smile and eye already glimmered with suppressed mischief. And I thought that I knew and liked the earlier Gladwell better than the later one.

She went off to fetch tea and I sat alone in my armchair and scanned the large dull room in which there wasn't an object out of place or a single book. No wonder she felt the lack of company. I was baffled as to how a person of Gladwell's flamboyance could have emerged from such a stultifying environment; though on reflection I supposed it was not so surprising. The more I thought about it, in fact, the more rebellion seemed the only answer.

Mrs Gladwell brought tea on a tray, in cups, not mugs, along with a china plate of petticoat tails. I wondered whether to consider myself especially honoured, or whether this was the way she always served it. Having set the tray down on the glass-topped coffee table she began to pour.

"So you and Ralph worked together for a number of years?" she said. "Milk?"

"Just a little, please. Two or three years. We—collaborated—sometimes."

"How nice. In that case you must have known him quite well. Sugar?"

"No, thanks. It's hard to say. I never felt he was a person you could fully know. If you get my meaning."

She handed me my cup. "No, I don't think I do."

"There was always something unknowable about him."

"Isn't that true of most people?" she said, smiling. She had very white, even teeth. "Please—have a biscuit."

"Thank you. Yes, but I suppose it was more true of Ralph than of anyone else. In my experience, that is."

"That must make the project you have in mind quite difficult."

"Yes. Yes, I suppose it does." I threw her a smile of my own. "I like a challenge."

She settled back in her armchair, crossed her legs and brought her cup to her lips. "I always thought Ralph the most transparent person in the world." After taking a sip she added, "But I am his mother."

"In that case, you are probably the most well-placed to help me," I said, still smiling.

"Or the worst. I feel quite protective of him, you see. Especially now."

"Of course. I understand that completely. There couldn't be any worse violation than—what happened to your son."

"Than to be murdered."

"Yes." I thought it best to let a few reverential moments pass. "Maybe that's why I feel so passionately about what I want to do. To speak up for Ralph now that he can no longer speak for himself. To defend him, somehow."

"Does he need defending?"

"Well," I said, "you must have read the newspapers." It suddenly occurred to me that she might not have been reading them. Under the circumstances, it would be understandable.

"I haven't been reading the newspapers," she responded curtly, and put down her teacup.

"I'm sorry. I'm not expressing myself well," I stammered. "When I said defend Ralph I didn't mean against criticism of any kind. I'm not sure what I mean except that as his friend and admirer I want to protect his literary legacy. For his work to be properly valued, rather than dismissed, as work of that nature can so easily be."

I was breathless with effort, but Mrs Gladwell remained oblivious.

"I don't understand about literature," she said.

"Precisely. That's entirely my remit. But you can help me more than you might realise, just by telling me about the Ralph you knew. Was he a clever child?"

"Enormously clever. He was a very, very clever child."

"Did he get on at school?"

"How do you mean?"

"Well, very gifted children don't always thrive. Sometimes the institutional framework is too confining for them."

"We couldn't afford a private education. Especially not after my husband passed away."

"Of course not. Please don't imagine I'm making a criticism. Any kind of school might have been restricting for a boy of Ralph's intellect. Or perhaps he enjoyed it? That's what I'm trying to find out."

She was silent, grim-faced; then she blurted out, "He hated school. Absolutely hated it."

"Why was that?"

"Well, he was too clever. As you've said. He was far too clever."

"He was frustrated, then?"

"I think so. And you know how unkind children can be."

"The other children made fun of him?"

"Well, he was tall and—unusual-looking. But he could make people laugh. He always knew how to do that."

"So making people laugh was his way of deflecting ridicule?"

"I suppose so."

"I imagine he read a lot as a child."

"Oh, yes. He was always reading." She added, "I've never been a reader. It was his father he took after. All the readers are on that side of the family."

"I see. Then it was your husband who encouraged him to read?"

"He didn't need any encouragement. He took to it like a duck to water. It must be something genetic on the Gladwell side."

"Your husband was a clever man?"

"Oh, he was very clever. He worked for the civil service."

"Were he and Ralph close?" I asked this out of pure curiosity.

"How do you mean, close?"

"Well. Did they play games together? Build model aeroplanes? Model railways? Anything like that?"

"Oh, no. Ralph never cared for any of those things."

"Just reading, then?"

"Reading and writing. He was always writing."

I leaned forward. "Really? What was he writing?"

"I don't know. I never read any of it."

"How come?"

"He wouldn't let me. He was very secretive. In any case, I wouldn't have wanted to read it."

"But you must have had some idea. Was it stories? Poetry?"

"Stories and poetry, I think. And longer things. Novels. Especially when he was a teenager. I think he wrote several novels."

I leaned back in my chair. My heart was pounding and my palms were damp. I replaced my cup in its saucer as carefully as I was able. "Mrs Gladwell. This is exactly the sort of material that would help me in my study. Do you think you could manage to lay your hand on any of it?"

"I don't know… Ralph was always so secretive, as I say."

"You wouldn't be betraying his trust. No-one could treat your son's work with greater respect than I."

"All the same… In any case, I don't know if I still have anything. He took most of his personal belongings with him when he left home."

"But he left some behind? Would it not be worth checking? I would be so enormously grateful."

She ran her palms over her knees and lifted her eyes to the ceiling. I raised my own instinctively.

"His room is still as he left it?" I inquired.

"Oh, no. It's been redecorated several times. Of course, it was still his room, not that he came back that often, but I always had a bed for him. Ralph knew that this would always be his home." A blush suffused her face, and her eyes welled up.

"Mrs Gladwell, I would be deeply honoured if you would allow me to see Ralph's room."

She turned her large, Ralphlike eyes on me. With their red rims and magnifying tears they were almost alarming. "Well, I don't know. I mean, I don't suppose there's any reason why not. It's a little strange."

"Honestly, there's nothing strange about it, I promise you. Any biographer would want to do the same. Who knows, maybe we'll discover something?" I tried to make this sound an exciting prospect, but feared I only came across as desperate. Could any stone really be left unturned in this neurotically tidy house?

"All right," she agreed, uncertainly. And she rose and led me back out into the hall.

As we mounted the stairs with their sage-green carpeting I felt to the heart of my bones the suffocating silence of this house in which Mrs Gladwell lived on the proceeds of her husband's life insurance, in which the ghosts of her husband and son surely couldn't survive, swept as they were from every cupboard and skirting-board; a house in which they couldn't bear to live, and so were hardly likely to return to dead. And yet the house was haunted, but by whom? By Mrs Gladwell herself, perhaps, and all the years of her well-kept loneliness.

Upstairs the doors were all closed, symbolically as it seemed to me, and the door to the left of the landing with its brass handle and its neat white panels appeared, like Gladwell himself, to be shut against me. But Mrs Gladwell swiftly opened it, and stepping aside, allowed me to enter the room I had rightly guessed, from the driveway, to belong to Ralph.

It was a smallish room, mostly filled by a double bed with a yellow chintz counterpane and a frilly valance, and made to feel smaller by the busy wallpaper. There was a pine bedside cabinet with a lamp and radio-alarm, a hard chair and a set of fitted wardrobes with sliding doors. A trapezoid of sunlight fell into the room, accentuating its silent emptiness, or more correctly, absence, the absence of any inhabiting personality. Gladwell, I perceived, had long since left the building.

"This is Ralph's room," Mrs Gladwell said. "As you can see, there isn't much left of his."

"But there is something?"

"That radio-alarm was his. He never much liked getting up for school. Or anything else, for that matter. He was a late sleeper."

I glanced at the drawers of the bedside cabinet, at the fitted wardrobes, at the frills of the valance behind which who knew what might lurk, and my fingers itched. If only she would leave me alone in here, I would have the place ransacked within fifteen minutes.

"You don't still have any of his books?"

"I doubt it. I'm sure he took all his books with him when he left."

"Mrs Gladwell. This is terribly important to me, as you can no doubt gather. Would you mind dreadfully if we checked the drawers and cupboards?"

A peculiar expression distorted her features, of mingled perplexity and—I thought—amusement. "Honestly, Mr Tate, I can assure you. There's nothing in the cupboards. But by all means check." She made a free gesture. This was all I needed. I slid back the doors of the wardrobe. A number of female garments in plastic mothproof covers filled the hanging space. There were several shelves, carefully organised into a medicine cabinet with labelled tupperware boxes. There wasn't a speck of dust or a morsel of fluff, although the room had the unused smell inevitable in a guest bedroom. I opened the drawers of the bedside cabinet. The top one held a packet of over-the-counter sleeping pills. The other two were empty. What the hell, I thought, and despite knowing it was pointless, I got down and lifted the valance and checked underneath the bed. There was nothing there.

"Mrs Gladwell," I said, sitting back on my haunches. "You said earlier that you thought Ralph the most transparent person in the world." It was the only interesting remark she had made. "Could you explain to me what you meant by that?"

"Well, I don't know. I suppose I always felt I knew him because he was so like his father."

"Really? In what way?"

"Sensitive. Anxious to please."

A snake of malice twisted in my chest.

"So innocent and hopeful, somehow. And then so disappointed. I always felt he was in need of protection. He was so vulnerable."

"Really?" I repeated. My tone must have been uglier than I intended, because she threw me a surprised, even mistrustful look. I got up off the floor. "Well. I think I've probably seen all there is to see."

She stared at me. I could feel myself getting warm. I needed to get out of that airless bedroom, out of that house. If I stayed there one more minute I would suffocate.

"I wonder if I might use your bathroom?" I said.

"Of course. It's across the landing." She wiped her eyes hastily. "I'll be downstairs."

I rushed across the landing and shut the door. There I lingered a few minutes in the gleaming bathroom, in which it appeared nobody had ever done anything so vulgar as to wash themselves or use the toilet. I stared into the mirror; never a good move, but I wanted to check my expression, look into my own eyes, reassure myself that there was no betrayal there. Mrs Gladwell might have been intellectually stupid, but she had plenty of emotional intelligence. I flushed the toilet and washed my hands unnecessarily.

Before returning downstairs I could not resist peeking behind the other doors on the landing. The master bedroom was in half-darkness, its bed neatly made, its curtains drawn. It gagged on chintz. A collection of gleaming objects stood on the dressing table, women's things, carefully arranged and thoroughly dusted; and there were more pictures, a framed wedding photograph (the young Barry's resemblance to Ralph was almost frightening) but none of Ralph himself. I closed the door softly and opened the final one to discover a small boxroom containing—somewhat to my disbelief—nothing at all.

I found Mrs Gladwell, her composure regained, perching on the sofa in the living room. She rose as I entered.

"Mrs Gladwell. You've been very kind. I hope my visit hasn't been too upsetting for you."

"I'm sorry I couldn't be of more assistance."

"Not at all. You've been a great help. I know how difficult it must have been for you."

"I'm not exactly myself at the moment."

"You're still in shock. It's perfectly understandable. I'm still in shock myself." Summoning all my sincerity I added, "I really miss him. As a colleague and a friend."

I must have sounded convincing, because she repeated with genuine feeling, "I wish I could be of more help." Then she said, "You know, most of Ralph's things are still in London. The police have been going through them, but at some point they'll be released back to us. I'm sure there must be masses of material you can make use of there."

"Yes. Yes, I'm sure there must."

"When the time comes, I'll get in touch."

"Thank you, Mrs Gladwell. That's extremely kind of you."

She opened the front door and let me out. I strode off down the driveway like a man released from prison into the fresh free air.

— VI —

THREE WEEKS PASSED BEFORE I heard back from Gladwell about my Katherine Mansfield parody, and then he didn't refer to the parody as such, but sent me another of his cryptic emails:

> *What do you think parody is for?*
> *G*

I took this as an implied criticism of my efforts, as if to say I had got it wrong somehow, I didn't know what parody was for and if I had, I would have written a better parody, a deeper and more meaningful one, one which lived up to Mansfield and to Gladwell. If I had succeeded in doing that he wouldn't even have needed to ask the question.

I was miffed, so I didn't answer him for a while. But I knew that he knew, with the confidence of the successful and established, that I wouldn't want to let go of this tenuous connection I had made, this gossamer thread of communication with my hero; so he could afford to sit back and leave me to stew in my juices. Nevertheless, I fought against my own impulse to reply. I lost myself in my day job (easily done, since my work was irritating and stressful), tried to forget about him, hoped that with the passing days I would lose the desire to write back altogether. All in vain. At every opportunity a continual argument ran through my head, in the lunch hour, on the ride home, as I made dinner, as to what precisely parody was for.

Eventually, after a week of both mental and actual drafting and redrafting (some of my answers were essays of several pages), I decided to mirror the master by replying as succinctly as he had asked:

To make people laugh.

The moment I had pressed Send I wished I had written:

What do you *think parody is for?*

That would have been so beautiful, so fine, so witty: a sort of parody in itself. A perfect mirror. But it was too late. Two months passed and I got no response.

I went back to my usual dull life and stopped thinking about parody. I even stopped visiting Gladwell's blog. Somehow I couldn't bear to look at it; even the sight of the home page reminded me of my own inadequacy. I was unworthy of his friendship. I couldn't write great literature and I couldn't even write good parody. I was a failure in every respect. I would never amount to anything.

Then it happened: the outrageous thing. After six or seven weeks I was almost weaned from the blog, but then, after a particularly difficult day when I was too tired for anything else I thought, Why the hell shouldn't I, what difference does it make whether I read it or not, I could do with a laugh. But I doubted whether, after what had happened between us, Gladwell would be able to make me laugh any more. And then my curiosity was really piqued, because I wanted to test my theory as to whether resentment and embarrassment could cancel laughter. So I navigated my way to his home page, that familiar page with its background of writers' faces caricatured and the name 'Gladwell the Parodist' scrawled across the top in spiky letters. And what should I find there but a parody of Katherine Mansfield.

It was not my parody, that is, not exactly or completely. But it contained enough ideas from my parody to be like a shadow or echo of it, a garment in which fragments of my cloth appeared. To be more precise: my parody formed the bones of Gladwell's parody.

Needless to say, I was livid. My first urge was to write and express my fury. In fact, that isn't quite true. My first urge was to stab him between the eyes. Since that option wasn't available, I jabbed out an hysterical email full of righteous indignation over what I called his "low, thieving and egregious plagiarism." Fortunately, I had the self-restraint not to send it. My initial anger blown off, I sat helplessly at my computer and wondered what to do.

I suppose at this point I should say a little more about myself, not by way of justification but purely in the interests of providing context. I am not by nature a volatile person, indeed I think of myself as rather phlegmatic, cautious and (as already mentioned) inclined to consult my second thoughts. Perhaps it is because of this that, when I do explode, the results are somewhat volcanic. In this I take after my father, the manager of a medium-sized branch of the Midland Bank who was made redundant in his mid-fifties and has never, I think, quite come to terms with the disappointment of his ambitions (these are vague and not, I believe, entirely connected either with the bank or with his boat, which he has spent the last twelve years of his life assiduously repainting but very rarely sailed). My mother is a sweet inoffensive woman. Maybe twice a year my father will lose his temper over some apparently trivial matter and break something, usually a piece of my mother's treasured china, or he will throw the TV remote at the coffee table and make a dent in it, much to my mother's distress, since she cares about these things; so that it seems he is taking his anger out on her although she is not the occasion of his fury. Once he snapped a hand-painted wooden salad spoon from Austria in two. He is always apologetic afterwards. It was partly as a result of witnessing my father's life of quiet desperation that I vowed to myself I would never work in a bank, but I cannot say I have entirely avoided it by going into arts administration. In any case, as I have matured I have noticed more and more similarities between myself and him, not least of which is this tendency to the occasional bout of fiery temper. Whether the causes are circumstantial or genetic I cannot say; probably a combination of both.

One thing I do know I have inherited from my parents is a strong sense of injustice, of right and wrong. The theft of ideas has always struck me as worse even than that of property. It is the invasion and ransacking of a person's mind, and more often than not, a violation of trust.

Hence my stormy reaction to what I discovered on Gladwell's blog; though as I say, I allowed myself to vent in private before settling down to consider how I should proceed. When I did write to Gladwell at last, it went as follows:

> *Great parody of Mansfield. Puts mine to shame. You were right, she is a tough nut to crack.*
> *Jim Tate*

Within twenty-four hours I received a reply from the egotistical old pirate.

> *Thanks. I love Mansfield. In a strange way you gave me permission to try her.*
> *I never answered your answer about parody. There's a lot more to it than making people laugh.*
> *G*

I said:

> *I realise that. I suppose I was just trying too hard to be succinct.*
> *Jim*

He said:

> *Always a danger. Of course, laughter is the* sine qua non. *The question is whether one writes parody in a spirit of love or hatred.*

I answered:

> *Both?*

To which he replied:

> *Yes, both. What do you look like, anyway, Jim Tate? Is there a photo?*

Gladwell must have been in a good mood. Maybe he was drunk. Maybe he was just happy. As for me, I was ecstatic. I was also terrified. All he needed was to see what I really looked like for his rejection to be instantaneous. So I mailed him a picture of an ancient Roman statue. I chose Antinous, the beautiful youth beloved of the Emperor Hadrian.

Very nice, Antinous, he answered. *I'm always in the Welly on a Wednesday evening.*

My joy was overwhelming. I could never have imagined it would be so easy.

— VII —

After my visit to Mrs Gladwell I bided my time for a few days, considering my next port of call. The police investigation was still ongoing, although I suspected at this point that the trail had gone cold; the last I'd heard was that they were checking CCTV footage from the local area. Since they didn't even know who they were looking for, that could keep them busy for a good long while.

I assumed they had been questioning Ralph's friends and lovers—those of them they could identify, at least—one by one. It was partly this that made me hesitate; I guessed that those who had been through one police interrogation wouldn't appreciate further probing from a nearly total stranger. The last thing I wanted was to get myself mixed up in the investigation, which had nothing whatever to do with my pursuit of Gladwell's manuscripts.

On the other hand, I sensed, time was of the essence. For all I knew, Gladwell had left instructions for his novels to be destroyed in the event of his death. I therefore decided to take the bull by the horns and approach the prince, the principal, that is, among all friends, all lovers, the Bosie to Gladwell's Wilde, the Patroclus to his Achilles: none other than Aaron Milner himself.

I had heard through the grapevine that Milner was back from his father's yacht, or wherever he had been, and sitting in his flat with the blinds drawn. That description may have been fanciful—there had also been sightings in several gay nightclubs, apparently—but I figured the flat would be my best bet. So I got dressed up in one of my smarter outfits, gelled and spiked my hair, what there was of it, applied a little aftershave and caught the tube to Knightsbridge.

I don't know why I felt the need to prettify myself, except that I was a bit in awe of Aaron solely on the grounds of his extreme good looks. I imagined that, like all good-looking people, he had no time for any but the beautiful. On the other hand, he was neither talented nor intelligent, which gave me back the advantage. At least, in my sharp suit and sharp hair, I need not feel totally ashamed of my appearance.

His opulent mansion flat was served by a uniformed doorman who, after letting me into the foyer, respectfully requested to know whether I had an appointment. I replied that I was a friend and had come to offer my condolences. The doorman asked, with an exquisite mix of the formal and the avuncular, if I would wait while he called up to Mr Milner. I sat on a deep leather chesterfield admiring the utterly bourgeois display of potted plants and marble flooring and art deco stained glass in the immaculate foyer while he telephoned from a small wrought iron booth without removing his gloves. In two minutes he emerged and told me that Mr Milner thanked me for my condolences but regretted he was not at home to visitors.

Thinking on my feet I replied, "Please would you tell Mr Milner that I have something belonging to him that I would like to return personally."

The doorman raised one eyebrow very slightly and

hesitated. I could see that he was making up his mind whether or not I was worth the trouble. I remained seated and looked coolly back at him. After a moment he returned to the little booth with just the merest air of someone reluctant to break protocol. It must have been hard for him to bother his rich employer twice in five minutes. When he returned, however, he asked with great courtesy if I would like to make my way up to the third floor.

Having successfully negotiated the first hurdle, I ascended in the old-fashioned lift. While I retained an outward appearance of calm self-confidence—the mirror on the back wall told me so—inside I was a trembling mass of nerves. Mrs Gladwell had been a piece of cake compared to this. She and I, after all, were cut from the same middle class cloth; we spoke the same language, more or less. Aaron Milner represented wealth, glamour, privilege: Eton, Oxford, the posh gay circuit, yachts, stately homes, celebrity parties. And yet he had fallen in love with, and married, a man as middle class as myself. That aberration of taste had shown, at least, that he was human.

Nevertheless, it was a situation calculated to inflame my always keen sense of inferiority. The way I was confronted, for example, when I stepped out of the lift, with a phalanx of imposing oak doors, none of which identified itself as being the entrance to the flat: in my paranoia I took this as being some kind of test only those of the right breeding would be able to pass, those used to frequenting Knightsbridge mansion flats. I hovered at a loss for a few moments in the windowless lobby where a large abstract painting, extraordinarily ugly and probably worth thousands, also hung. Eventually I picked a door and knocked, and after a few seconds Aaron opened a door behind me. It was all arranged to make me feel like an idiot.

"You?" he said, and didn't let me in for the moment.

"Jim Tate," I confirmed, holding out my hand. He ignored it, and stood staring at me with a puzzled, impatient expression, as though he had expected to see somebody else. I dropped my hand, suppressing a rising feeling of annoyance. "I was a friend of Ralph's."

"I saw you around. I think." He continued to seem puzzled, perhaps trying unsuccessfully to place me, but stepped aside and allowed me into the flat.

The interior was in entire contrast to both the foyer and the claustrophobic little lobby. The reception room we first entered—one of several, I imagined—was huge, and although the fabric was Victorian, it had been made over in an ultra-modern style. There was a charcoal carpet, grey-and-chrome furniture and a selection of large abstract paintings in silver and orange which looked as though the artist had simply taken a decorator's brush and flung it two or three times against a blank canvas. It wasn't true that the blinds were drawn, but the tall windows were hung with gauze curtains which admitted a soft light while rendering the outside world a hazy blur.

"I wanted to offer you my condolences in person," I said.

Milner was no longer looking at me. He seemed distracted; I was surprised by how bad he appeared. He was, always had been beautiful, of course, in a sulky male model way, and at thirty-two it required no effort for him to remain so. But he was borderline scruffy in his rumpled chinos and thin grey designer t-shirt, his blond hair uncombed, and there were shadows under his eyes I had not seen before. He must really have been grieving.

Just then his mobile phone buzzed, and he whipped it out of his pocket and checked the screen. Without excusing himself or inviting me to sit down he stood there texting. I had always disliked him, and though I knew this behaviour was no more than was usual nowadays—in fact it was generally considered the height of good manners—at this particular moment it made my blood boil. But I remained patiently standing, with perhaps the ghost of a good-natured smile at the corners of my lips.

When at last he had finished, at least for the time being, he slipped his phone back into his pocket and said, without preamble, "You said you had something of mine."

I nodded. "I thought it would be better if I gave it to you myself, rather than entrusting it to the post." He looked at me expectantly. "Do you mind if we sit down a moment?"

He was all impatience; he clearly wanted me to give him whatever it was right away and then get out of his life, but I had no intention of satisfying him so fast, or at all, if it came to that. We adjourned to the L-shaped sofa, whose vast grey acreage gave us ample scope to keep our distance, but after allowing him to sit first, I sat down about two feet away.

"I've been finding the last few weeks pretty strange," I began.

"Tell me about it."

"Yeah. I guess they've been more than pretty strange for you."

"Try pretty fucking strange. Fucking journalists on my tail the whole fucking time. Fucking police. I was their number one suspect. Fucking charming." He took out and lit a cigarette. He didn't offer me one, not that I would have accepted.

"It must have been awful. I'm sorry."

"Well, I got the fuck out of the country. It was the only answer."

I knew he must have provided an alibi. They surely would not have let him leave England otherwise. "It must have been quite difficult, coming back."

He shrugged. Then he looked at me with that puzzled expression again, puffing away and blowing smoke in my face, as if trying afresh to place me. "I saw you in Heaven."

I shook my head. "The Welly, more likely. I'm no clubber."

"No. All right. It must have been the Welly." He turned away and tapped ash into a black granite ashtray, big and heavy enough to brain a man. He was not terribly interested. How could someone like me possibly interest someone like him? He gazed off into the curtains, distracted again, and from the gleam in his eye seemed to be remembering. An expression of deep sadness scudded across his face.

"You must miss him," I said as gently as I could.

"What?" He turned back to me. "I dunno. It's confusing. It's not like we were even together any more."

"Yes, but… you can still miss him. I mean, it's not like he was a big part of my life, but he was big in himself—you know? I feel like something massive has disappeared." I gazed at my knees, aware I was walking a tightrope, judging my next step word by word, moment by moment. And yet I had no idea where the tightrope led; only what it was I so badly wanted.

"Yes, well. Ralphie had that effect on people."

"There's a difference between him being gone and elsewhere and being gone and—gone. You know?"

"Yeah." He stood and walked away, and remained with his back to me, his face to the window. I thought he might be trying to hide the fact that he was on the verge of tears. "What pisses me off is, all the people who used to slag him off are talking about him now like he was Saint Francis of Assisi or something. You know? I mean, the fucking hypocrites! Ralphie was never easy, he was a fucking sarcastic bastard, but I always respected him. Even after we split up I respected him. But these people! I mean, he was *murdered*. I can't get my head round it. Somebody *murdered* him."

I have to confess I was taken aback. I hadn't believed Milner capable of so much unselfish feeling.

"It's beyond shocking," I agreed.

"I blame myself. If I'd been there… We would have been back together within six weeks." He wheeled round all of a sudden. His eyes were red-rimmed. "So what were you to him, anyway? Not one of his *boys*, I can see that much."

His expression of mingled dismissal and distaste made him quite ugly. I swallowed the morsel of sympathy I was beginning to feel for him. "We worked together."

"*Worked* together? That's a laugh. Ralphie never did a stroke of work in his life. You mean at the university?"

"No. On the blog. We collaborated sometimes."

"You're kidding me. Ralphie never collaborated with anyone."

"I was very much the junior partner," I said with as much modesty as I could muster.

"He didn't need a junior partner."

"All the same. That's what happened. I came up with ideas and he used them."

"Why would he want to do that?"

"I had good ideas. Maybe he was getting tired."

He stared at me for a few moments as though he were considering me in a new light. "Maybe," he said. "Maybe he was getting tired. Maybe that's what went wrong for us."

"Listen," I said. "My relationship with Ralph was entirely literary."

Much to my annoyance, Milner responded with a snort of laughter. "You don't say!"

I smiled, to humour him. "It was entirely literary, celibate, cerebral, whatever you want to call it, and perhaps for that reason I feel I have a vested interest, perhaps the only pure interest in protecting and promoting his literary legacy."

"Eh?"

"I want to make sure his achievement isn't lost. That his name isn't forgotten."

"That's a joke. How exactly do you intend to do that?"

"By writing a book about him."

"Whoa! Stop right there." He held up a palm, and reached down swiftly to stub out his cigarette. "I think we've come to the end of this conversation."

"I don't mean dish the dirt. Not a biography. It's going to be solely and purely about his work."

"Sounds like it'll be a million-seller." Having killed his cigarette, he bounced back to his spot before the window with jaunty athleticism. I felt like hitting him. But I only smiled.

"I'm not interested in making money," I said, with perfect honesty. "I'm only interested in literature."

"Oh, in *leetretchure*."

"In parodic literature, to be specific. It's an art form I feel has never received its due."

"Isn't that kind of the point?" he replied, startling me with a sudden moment of insight. He was quite right, of course. Parody was the mirror in which seriousness was reflected and shown to be ridiculous. If parody were to be taken seriously the whole palace of literature would begin to fall apart.

I decided to cut to the chase. "Why do you think Ralph wrote parody rather than trying his hand at novels or poetry of his own?"

"You mean, why did he write parody rather than the stuff that gets parodied?" He chuckled in fond remembrance. "Because he was bright! Because he was brilliant! Because he had a better sense of humour!" Milner walked over to one of the sleek grey cupboards and popped it open to reveal a well-stocked bar. Somewhat to my astonishment, since it was only eleven o'clock in the morning, he began mixing himself a cocktail. "Anyway," he added, "he'd already tried all that crap."

My ears pricked up. I did my best not to show it. "All what crap?"

"Novels, poetry. Novels mainly. I think he'd already written half a dozen."

"Really? Did he ever try to publish them?"

"Did he ever! He showed me a wad like this of rejection slips." He measured a very thick sandwich with his hands. "He read some of them aloud and we laughed like drains. What a bunch of wankers!" Appropriately, at this juncture he began jigging the cocktail shaker back and forth.

"So he turned his hand to parody out of disappointment?"

"No, it wasn't out of *disappointment*. Fuck that. It was out of revenge." He strained the bright blue mixture into a martini glass. It didn't seem to cross his mind to offer me any. He returned to the sofa and sat down at a distance, glass in hand.

"What is that?" I asked.

"Gloomchaser," he replied, sipping. It failed to live up to its name, evidently; he looked more miserable with each sip he took.

"So he was taking his revenge on literature?" I continued.

"Yup. On literature and the wankers who peddle it."

"I see... What about those novels of his? Did you ever read them?"

"Bits of them. Bits of some of them. He read me some bits."

"What did you think? Were they any good?"

"They were hilarious."

"Intentionally or unintentionally?"

"Fuck knows! Intentionally, I suppose. They made *me* laugh."

"What about Ralph—did they make him laugh?"

"I dunno. I can't remember. We were probably drunk or stoned. What difference does it make?"

"No difference. I'm just curious." All the difference in the world, I thought. "What were they about?"

"Sex, mainly. Leastways, the bits he read to me were all about sex." He laughed suddenly, lasciviously, grimly, and swigged his drink. "They were filthy!"

My palms were sweating. I ran them down my thighs. "What happened to the manuscripts? Do you know?"

"He always told me he planned to burn them one day. And destroy the disks."

"Did he?"

"Of course not. You know how vain Ralphie was about his work. He couldn't bring himself to singe a single precious page." Aaron knocked back the rest of his gloomchaser and got up to refill his glass at the bar. "He always asked me to promise to destroy them after his death." He paused, stared into the mirror at the back of the bar, then went on pouring. "If he died before me, that is."

"And did you?"

"Did I what?"

"Did you promise him?"

"Of course."

"And?"

"And what?"

"Did you burn them?"

He returned to the sofa and sat down with one leg folded under the other. He already seemed slightly drunk. Maybe this wasn't his first cocktail of the day. "How could I do that? The police impounded everything. I haven't even been able to enter his place."

"Then he didn't leave them with you?"

"No." He looked and sounded annoyed. "What the fuck is this? Some sort of Nazi interrogation?"

My urgency had got the better of me. I'd been pushing too hard, as I'd feared I might. Plough through, plough through, I told myself. Partial honesty is the best policy. "Well, I would like to see them, of course. If I'm to write a literary study then they'd be essential reading."

Fortunately, he was satisfied with this ruse of mine. "Oh. Well, you can't. The police probably have them. And fuck knows when they'll ever release his stuff."

This was a blow. Milner had been my best hope. But I kept my apparent equanimity. "That's a real shame," I sighed. "I guess I'll have to be patient. You don't have anything else that would be of interest?"

He stared at me with those red eyes. His grief was raw. I shuddered. "Like what?"

"I don't know. Poems. Letters. You tell me."

"I'm not showing you any fucking poems or letters."

"No. No, of course not. No harm in asking. But in case you change your mind—" I dug into a pocket, fished out one of my cheap, fake business cards and gave it to him. He took it disbelievingly, as though I had handed him a small turd.

I stood up. "Well. Thank you very much for your time." But he made no move to see me to the door. Instead he went on sitting there with his glass in his hand and those blazing red eyes staring up at me, accusingly as it seemed, though that could just have been my own paranoia.

"You said you had something of mine."

Shit. I'd hoped he would forget about that. "Yes. Yes, all right." I plunged a trembling hand into my pocket. "I believe this is yours." I passed him the cigarette lighter, a vintage one with a fleur-de-lys motif. He took it from me with an expression of naked pain.

"Where did you get this?"

"I found it."

He turned it over and over in his hand, staring at it as though it were the murder weapon itself. "No, you fucking didn't." He jumped up suddenly and seized me by the lapel. "Where did you get it?" he demanded again.

"I told you," I gasped. "I found it. At the Welly. He left it behind on one of the tables there."

He let go then and moved away, still turning the lighter in his fingers and gazing at it with a haunted, abstracted look. "Get out," he said.

"All right."

"Get the fuck out of my home."

"I'm going." I made for the door, but some demon made me pause on the threshold and add, "Thank you so much for seeing me. It's been really helpful. Parody as revenge. I never would have got that otherwise."

"Get *out*!" His teeth were bared, and as he leapt toward me I dashed out of the door. Not daring to linger to mess about with the lift, I ran as fast as I could down the service staircase.

— VIII —

I TOOK THE TUBE to Soho straight from work, and arrived at the Duke of Wellington around six o'clock, early enough to install myself unobtrusively in a corner near the entrance. From there I watched intently all the comings and goings, convinced of my ability to recognise Gladwell, when he appeared, by a sort of sixth sense. A lot of pretty young men in tight t-shirts greeted one another with hugs and cries of joy, and there were a fair number of business suits, unwinding before the tube ride home to the suburbs, where they lived, doubtless, in overpriced Victorian workers' cottages full of stripped floorboards and stainless steel kitchens. It was a warm summer's evening, and a lively crowd built up, spilling outside onto the pavement and into the square.

I drank orange juice; no-one approached or even noticed me. I realised a long time ago that I am not the sort of person others register, or if they do, it is only to find me repulsive. This bothered me once; but no longer. When they turn their backs, I let myself in. I have sharp eyes, sharp hearing and I have made a fine art out of my ability to eavesdrop.

Around seven thirty, a small but talkative group of men entered and went straight upstairs. This piqued my interest immediately, but what really caught my attention was the fact that one of them was well over six feet tall. I had seen Gladwell referred to online as Bigfoot and, occasionally, Heap Big Chief, and I guessed his long hair—greying, tied back in a ponytail with a leather thong—had suggested the Red Indian connection. I slid from my seat and, orange juice in hand, quietly followed them up.

The first floor was less crowded, understandably so, as most of the clientele preferred to be outside, but there were enough people up there to camouflage my presence. The talkative group had settled themselves in a corner that was clearly theirs, and the tall man presided not only because of his height but by means of his presence, a sort of kingly aura he gave off which made everyone around him seem subject. It was the closest I had ever come to someone possessed of that innate, indefinable quality known as charisma.

Drinks were brought up on a tray, and the group went on talking and laughing. It was hard to make out individual conversations, but I surmised from their tone and their hand gestures that they were not discussing football or foreign holidays. Politics possibly, literature perhaps; their expressions were at times quite intense, but every so often came a pulse of laughter. As for the tall man, I couldn't decode him at all. His voice was deep, but too soft to make out, and in my frustration I risked moving closer.

"Parodies of the Bible are without exception puerile," I heard him say, and I knew that he was Gladwell, "and always in poor taste."

The young man seated opposite, who had springy black hair and a pointed face, leather bracelets and a white wine spritzer, replied, "Surely poor taste is part of the job description?"

"I won't take that personally!" Gladwell chuckled.

"No; I refuse to trespass in the halls of genius. I will not parody Shakespeare. I will not parody the Bible. God wrote the Bible. And who is a greater genius than God?"

There was general laughter. Suddenly everyone was listening.

Gladwell continued, "There are only two motives for parody: envy and exposure. Now, in a work of genius there is nothing to envy and nothing to expose. Do I envy Shakespeare? No, I only love Shakespeare. When I was twenty-nine years old I envied Shakespeare for about five minutes. I remember the occasion clearly. I was riding home on the tube one evening when I suddenly realised I would never be able to surpass the Bard. You might say that twenty-nine was rather late for such a revelation, but I was extremely ambitious and deeply deluded in those days." More laughter. "When the truth suddenly struck me I felt a terrible pang, like a knife in my heart, and for several minutes I resented Shakespeare the way a small child kicks and screams when his mother won't let him have sweets. But I got over it very quickly and then all I felt was a great love and gratitude that something as wonderful as Shakespeare existed to inspire someone as lost and benighted as myself." Gladwell smiled, and so did his acolytes. "Any attempt to parody Shakespeare would not only be profoundly disrespectful, it would certainly fail to impress. Now, on the other hand, you have those writers whom everyone calls geniuses and who are simply begging to be exposed. Take Dickens, for example. Dickens was not a genius, he was a very hard-working hack, added to which, he had far too high an opinion of himself. But he is regarded as a genius because he so perfectly embodies *English Literature* and the comfortable English *social conscience* which loves to see how we have oppressed people in the past and then exonerated ourselves by nobly condescending to improve their lot. And we love Christmas, of course, which Dickens invented, and caricature and the grotesque, which are fatally easy to do, and sentimentality, which is fatally easy to do, all of which passes for art the way those tedious paintings of eighteenth century toffs on their country estates still do. And I should know, my parents' house was full of them." He took a mouthful of beer. "Dickens is the very embodiment of middlebrow philistinism, complete with a *moral message*. But he was no more capable of portraying a genuine emotion or a flesh-and-blood person than I am of writing like Shakespeare. Which is why he is so ripe for parody. I refer you to my various parodies of Dickens if you doubt me."

"But don't you envy him?" someone inquired.

"Apparently, he is immortal. I'm bound to envy him that. Why would I bother to parody a writer we have forgotten? It's the certain knowledge that I myself will be forgotten that drives me to ridicule the work of those unjustly remembered, or in the case of writers still living, undeservedly adulated in their own time. Of course, I run a small risk of being adulated and remembered myself, but at least I can remain secure in the knowledge that no-one is ever going to parody a parodist."

This brought a gale of laughter, and Gladwell swept up his half-drunk pint with the air of a man happily in command of a due measure of recognition and regard.

"Actually, that isn't entirely true, because Pope parodied Chaucer, and Isaac Hawkins Browne parodied Pope. But if you write nothing but parody, as I am proud to do, you can be certain that no-one will ever parody your parodies, which is why you will reign supreme and untouchable, even if you are forgotten. You can rest easy in your grave, knowing that you made your small contribution to the betterment of Art, and that you yourself will never be ridiculed."

I listened intently.

"Some people feel sorry for the parodist," Gladwell went on, "thinking him nothing but a disappointed wannabe venting his spleen on those more talented than himself. Nothing could be farther from the truth. What we must never forget is that the goal of the parodist is to make us laugh, and a good parodist will always bring a smile to our lips. A bad one will not, and that is when we only taste the bitterness of his spleen. How does a good parodist provoke laughter? By exposing the tics and absurdities and hypocrisies of the great, but often in a gentle way, a loving way, so that our laughter is sweet, or perhaps I should say sour-sweet, as when we recognise the frailties of human nature that we all have in common. The parodist is not bitter against literature, the parodist loves literature, maybe more than anybody else. But with his superior understanding of human nature he picks apart its finest threads and dismantles its most delicate machinery."

The gentleman doth protest too much, I thought. If there is one thing he is afraid of, it is ridicule. And if there is anything he is full of, it is bile and bitterness. Yes, even hatred. The goal of the parodist is to make us laugh! Even now he plagiarises my thoughts and repeats them as his own.

I snatched up my glass, but in my preoccupation I had failed to notice it was empty. But I couldn't leave right now. I remained where I was, my head bent and my ear attuned, keeping as still and unobtrusive as possible. I wanted to know who these people were who surrounded him. Were they really the slavish followers they seemed to be, or was there a spark of combativeness in any of them? Did any have the wit or intelligence to knock him off his pedestal from time to time? I longed to join the fray, but I knew my limitations. I am not a talker. If I had made myself known to Gladwell, he would have thought me not only ugly, but stupid. The sole hope I had of winning his admiration—or anyone else's, for that matter—was through my writing.

The young man with the pointed face said, "But are you then saying that any writer who takes themselves seriously deserves to have their bubble burst?"

Gladwell set down his drink, and cocked his head consideringly. But I knew he had thought this all through a thousand times and wasn't really considering anything. "Whether he deserves it or not, it is going to happen. That's the price you pay for going public. It isn't my job to take pity on people. Leave that to the reviewers!" He laughed, and the rest laughed with him. "No, sweet Anwar, believe me, I respect the deep seriousness of the artistic quest. I've no time for writers who don't take themselves seriously. It's the ones who make a mockery of Art who deserve my mockery."

"But you've parodied Virginia Woolf. Surely she doesn't make a mockery of Art?"

"I have the greatest respect for Virginia Woolf. But she lays herself open in all sorts of ways, by being a snob, by having tics of style, by taking herself too seriously and having no sense of humour. The surest way to deflect the laughter of others is to laugh at yourself first."

Anwar nodded, but I could tell he was not fully

convinced. And nor was I. However, the conversation broke up after that, and Gladwell turned to the man next to him and began gossiping about something.

I watched Anwar for a little while. He looked very young—maybe twenty-one or twenty-two—and was probably a student. I recognised the intense, earnest air of someone still finding their way. I was only just emerging from that phase of life myself, and I empathised. In Anwar's place I would not have had the wherewithal to tear down Gladwell's argument and make him see himself for what he was.

The evening progressed, and the group around the corner table grew more raucous as they got drunker. I felt glad to be out of it. I wandered down to the bar and refreshed my drink. Outside, the light began to fade and the t-shirted young men drifted away from the lawns and benches of the square where they had been lounging. Soon it was night, and I was getting tired; my sense of loneliness was oppressive, but whenever I felt someone notice me, I hunched reflexively into myself. Still I lingered, waiting for the party to descend. About eleven o'clock they did so, at least, there were Gladwell and Anwar, pulling on their jackets and talking on their way downstairs. I followed them discreetly as they exited the pub, leaving my umpteenth orange juice half-finished, and walked behind at a short distance as they made their way to the tube.

It was chucking-out time, and the station was busy with refugees from the pubs. I had a job on to keep up with my quarry. Gladwell on his long legs cut through the crowds like a pair of scissors, and Anwar was clearly accustomed to matching his pace. I only just managed to slip into their same carriage on the Northern Line. I sat down, panting. The two men were a bare three seats away from me, and I noticed with a shudder Gladwell's hand stroke Anwar's leg surreptitiously. They didn't speak. As the train drew in to Tufnell Park they got up all of a sudden, causing me to start; I was used to remaining on board for several further stops. I watched them to the doors, then hopped off after them. I had broken out in a cold sweat. There was no doubt in my mind that they were oblivious, but it was a while since I had done anything of this kind, and my heart was pounding.

Outside it was a warm, muggy London night and there were plenty of people milling about to provide me with cover. When the pair turned off down a quiet residential street I followed without a break in step, even though it was otherwise deserted. They never looked round or suspected anything. They held hands for a little while and once Gladwell murmured something to his young friend and softly laughed. Eventually they came to a tall brick terraced house and entered via the garden gate. Gladwell ran up the short flight of steps to the front door and inserted his key in the lock. I walked on swiftly by as though headed somewhere of my own.

A few seconds later I spun round and returned to the house in question. They had disappeared inside and the door had shut behind them. The blinds were closed but I was in time to see the lights come on. I remained standing on the pavement for perhaps five minutes, screened by a lilac bush, from behind which I observed glimmers of movement between the curtains, and eventually, with a pang, the lights going on upstairs.

Then I headed back to the tube station and got back

on the train which carried me to the further and cheaper reaches of the Northern Line, but not without first taking note of both the house number and the name of the street. The knowledge gave me a deep, obscure satisfaction, and I felt a sense of power and excitement I hadn't experienced in a long time.

— IX —

I HAD COME UP empty from my visits to both Gladwell's mother and his ex-husband, and was at something of a loss where to turn next. If they were not in possession of the manuscripts I desired so intensely it was hard to conceive who might be. He was hardly likely to have entrusted them to some casual friend.

Then again, it was just the sort of thing he might have done. Gladwell was nothing if not a master of misdirection. Until he met me, he had done nothing, so far as I could make out, but tell lies about himself, even to his supposedly nearest and dearest. I was the only person in whom he had ever confided the full truth. It would be just like him to leave his novels with somebody no-one would ever think of consulting, one of his many fuck-bunnies, for instance, some bellboy or construction worker who never read books, who had no idea he was even a writer.

In that case, they would probably never be found. But I couldn't allow my thoughts to run that way. Everything would dissolve into entropy and I would go insane. I must continue to be systematic. I sat down with a cup of cocoa and consulted my list of Gladwell's friends and acquaintances. In fact it was not so much a list as an intricate spider's web of interconnected contacts. It had taken me a long time to build up sufficient knowledge to create this diagram, and I still had to icism to protect their inner, vulnerable selves and both essentially regarded themselves as failures. It takes one to know one, as the saying goes, and Ralph and Ray had each other's number to the extent that they could inflict mutual wounds that were all but deadly. In fact, when it came to Ralph's murder, I wouldn't have been surprised if Marriner were one of Scotland Yard's chief suspects.

On the face of it, Ray was the last man to whom Ralph was likely to entrust his precious manuscripts. If they were, as I suspected them to be, works aspiring toward High Art, Marriner was just the person to relish their bloody vivisection. Having once read them, he would never give Gladwell another moment's peace or safety. He would sink his fangs in his friend's jugular at every opportunity.

Yet, on the other hand, there was a strange twinship between these vain, desperate men which meant they were just as capable of tenderly binding one another's wounds as they were of inflicting them. It was possible that Marriner was the one person Gladwell *would* trust to take care of his true literary legacy, whether to burn it as per his instructions or to ensure its survival until some future, more appreciative era. I decided to call on him at his Brick Lane studio without further delay.

The studio apartment was housed in one of those converted warehouses, anonymous and industrial-looking from the outside, which were so fashionable with artistic arrivistes. Situated down a littery sidestreet lined with taxicab companies and garment sweatshops, it retained its original battered door, let into the larger warehouse entrance, with a series of old iron buzzers beside it. According to instructions (Ray had agreed to meet with me when I made contact through his agent, and seemed quite ready to speak about his dead friend, which was a good start) I pressed the top buzzer and the man himself opened up to me, dressed in paint-spattered jeans and sweatshirt. At the first sight of me he did a double-take, as I'd expected, and seemed to be trying to place me as we exchanged greetings. Ignoring his puzzlement, I stepped over the high threshold.

Inside, the building was just as anonymous and industrial-looking as it had been from without. This surprised me; I had expected some highly expensive transformation of minimalist splendour. We mounted a set of dirty concrete steps lined with faded and peeling walls which didn't appear to have been renovated since the place had last closed for business. The windows of thick frosted glass were grimy and hung with cobwebs. On the third floor we passed through a bare plywood door and into a wide, open space, lit by a long row of opaque skylights, whose floor and walls were just as shabby but which was obviously the artist's studio. Numerous artworks in various stages of completion were scattered about, there were objects covered in dust sheets and several pieces of machinery which for all I knew were leftovers from the building's factory days, but more likely formed part of a contemporary artist's essential equipment.

At one end of the studio there stood a couple of old sofas and an electric fire, and behind a partition wall, as I was soon to discover, was a primitive kitchen: a microwave, a ring, a metal sink and a couple of units which looked like they had been filched from somewhere and never properly installed. It was a far cry from the millionaire artist's pad I had anticipated, but then Marriner was not a millionaire, and even if he had been, I quickly realised this was the kind of deprivational chic artists of his kind favoured when they were at work.

My host stepped straight through to the kitchen as he offered me refreshment—"Tea, coffee, vodka?"—and when I shrugged non-committally reached into one of the wonky cupboards and fetched out a bottle of twelve-year-old Scotch. "If we're going to talk about Ralph, this is probably required." From the draining board he swept two school tumblers which were clearly kept there for just such a purpose. He stalked out to the sofa, threw himself down and began pouring.

"I've seen you somewhere before, haven't I?" he said.

"Probably at the Welly. I used to come to the Wednesday night dos sometimes." I sat down on the other sofa and took the proferred glass although I loathe whisky.

"No, it wasn't the Welly. You've never sat round that table at the Welly." He fixed me with his beady little eye, evidently determined to place me somewhere. I leaned back, trying not to appear uncomfortable. Let him place me where he pleased; like everyone else, he would prove too unobservant ever to work it out.

"I came to your exhibition at the Directory."

"Yeah—and?"

"I liked it."

"That's not where I saw you, though."

"What did Ralph think of it?" I pursued, eager to change the subject.

"Who knows? Ralph would never be honest about what he thought. He probably didn't know himself. That man's psyche was a rabbit warren."

"What did he tell you?"

"He said he liked it. He could always afford to be generous to artists."

"Because he didn't feel competitive with them?"

"Exactly."

"But he was competitive with you."

"Only on an intellectual level. He always needed to win our arguments."

"And if he couldn't he would resort to blows."

"Sometimes." He looked at me carefully again. "You were there for that, then? Our scuffle at the Welly?" I nodded. "I could have killed him that evening, and I can't even remember what we were fighting about." He swallowed some whisky. "I guess I shouldn't say things like that, given what happened."

I held my glass of whisky but didn't drink it.

"The police thought I did it—did you know that? And I didn't even have an alibi. But I don't think they suspect me any more."

"How come?"

He laughed. "No real murderer would be as up front about himself as I am. I never do anything but tell the truth. That's the big difference between me and Ralph. Was the big difference, I should say. I can't lie, and he was incapable of being honest."

"Why do you think that was?"

"Because he hated himself so much. I never met anyone who hated themselves as much as he did." He drained his glass, topped it up and offered me the bottle. I declined. "I used to twist the knife. Now I just feel sorry for him. Poor Ralph." After a moment of reflection, he added, "It doesn't surprise me that he was murdered, though."

"Really?"

"No. He wanted people to hate him as much as he

did himself. My theory is, he pushed someone into killing him because he was too much of a coward to commit suicide."

"Jesus."

"I know. It's wild, isn't it. But Ralph had a real death-wish, I can tell you that."

I was silent for a few minutes. I swallowed some whisky without even realising I was doing so. It made me nearly gag. "Did you tell the police your theory?"

"Sure. I always tell people everything I think."

"And how did they take it?"

"They were very interested."

"I'll bet they were." I took another swig, this time consciously, and screwed up my mouth. It tasted like engine oil.

"They wanted to know if Ralph was into S&M. I said he might have been, but it wasn't something I knew anything about. It's years since we slept together, and he never wanted anything kinky as far as I recall. And you always had to take anything he said on the subject with a large pinch of salt." I made a mental note to do the same with Marriner's testimony from now on. I had tailed them to their hotel not more than a year ago. "Were you and he fucking?" he asked, blandly.

"No."

"Oh, well, I guess you wouldn't know, then."

"Our relationship was purely professional."

To my annoyance, Marriner laughed at this. "All right! If you say so. I don't know of any professional friend of Ralph's he didn't also fuck, but I imagine he could make an exception for you," and he looked me up and down in a way that made me want to hit him. I turned away toward the artworks scattered about the studio.

"What are you working on at the moment?" I asked.

"Funnily enough, a bust of Ralph. Want to see it?" I nodded. We got up and he led me over to a dust sheet-covered object on a trestle. He removed the sheet to reveal a tangle of wires, both metal and electrical, wound together with dried withies, red leather straps and various machine parts into a form the size and roughly the shape of a human head. It looked random at first, but the longer I examined it the more I seemed to see eye-sockets, a nose, even a mouth, but these altered depending on the angle from which they were observed, appearing by turns hopeful, angry, sardonic, mournful, dead.

"It's excellent," I said.

"It isn't finished yet."

"No, but I can see Ralph in it. The way you've captured so many faces. It's very clever."

"Well, they talk about people being two-faced. But Ralph was multi-faced. Wasn't he?"

I didn't reply. I stared at the bust. Marriner stared at me.

"Are you really planning to write a piece about Ralph?" he asked. "Or is it something else you're after?"

"Like what?"

"You tell me." He drew the dust sheet once more over the sculpture, and deprived of an object, I was obliged to return his gaze.

"I don't know what else you think I could be interested in."

"You could be pursuing your own investigation. Some amateur-sleuth-style attempt to find the murderer."

I smiled.

"So—what do you think?" he persisted. "Do you think I did it?" And he confronted me theatrically, striking a pose.

"Not for a minute."

"Oh." He seemed disappointed. "Why not?"

"Because I believe you loved Ralph too much. As a friend," I added swiftly. "I don't imagine you'll find another like him."

He dropped his pose, and his expression fell. "You're right. I'm going to miss him terribly." I remained silent. I wasn't of a mood to tell that lie. Swigging from his already empty glass, he flung himself back down onto the sofa. I approached and stood over him.

"There is something I am interested in, though," I continued.

He picked up the near-empty whisky bottle and sloshed some into his glass. "Oh, what's that?"

"His novels."

"His what?"

"Gladwell wrote some novels. I'd like to read them."

"First I've heard of it." He failed to look up at me, which aroused my suspicions.

"It's true. When he was younger, he wanted passionately to be a great novelist." I watched him drink, the liar. "He never showed you anything?"

"Not that I recall. I can't blame him. I'd have ribbed him mercilessly."

"I'm sure you would." I sat down. "You've really no recollection?"

He seemed to think about it. I watched his face carefully. "Nope. I'm coming up empty. Shame. I'd have liked to see a novel by Ralph. It would have been hilarious."

"Or it might have been deeply serious."

"Which means it would have been hilarious. Have you tried asking anybody else? Aaron, for example?"

"I'm working my way through the list."

"Oh, I see. Well, I'm sorry I can't help you."

We were both silent awhile. I learned a long time ago that if you keep quiet, the other person will usually feel bound to speak. Sure enough, Ray did so after a few minutes.

"You know, I took the piss out of Ralph no end while he was alive. But now that he's dead I feel kind of protective of him. I hope you aren't intending to tear him down."

"Even though he did it to other people?"

"Ah, that wasn't what Ralphie was about, at all."

"No?" I couldn't keep the edge out of my voice.

"No." He turned the whisky bottle upside down and drained the last drops into his waiting glass. "He was trying to help them. Really, he was trying to save them from themselves. I should know, because that's all I'm ever trying to do as well. Ralph and I understood that about each other."

I remained motionless, my barely touched glass upon the low table before me. He would never have guessed what fist of cold anger was beating in my chest.

"I would never normally say anything so sentimental," Marriner went on, "but the circumstances and all… You know what I mean. I really want to see him receive justice."

I almost laughed out loud. The justice I had in mind was so utterly unlike any he might have imagined. But I controlled myself. "What can I tell you? I can only do my level best," I said.

Marriner hesitated a while, then said, "There might be somebody else who could help you, but I've no idea how you might find him. The person Ralph was seeing at the end of his life. After Aaron left him."

My heart seemed to miss several beats. "I didn't think there was anyone after Aaron."

"Don't be a little girl. Of course there was." He wiped his nose on the back of his hand. "Actually, not a lot of people knew about it. Which is extraordinary, considering the amount of gossip that was always flying around. But Ralph was getting quite secretive towards the end. I don't know why. Are you drinking that?"

"What? Er—no…" I handed over my glass, and he poured the contents haphazardly into his own. "So, who was this person?"

"I've no idea, except that his name was Tim, or Timmy, or Timothy. Something like that."

"You met this person?" I asked, though I knew the answer.

"No, I never did. Ralph mentioned him when he was drunk a couple of times."

"He could have been just—you know—passing trade."

He laughed through his teeth. "What a quaint little man you are! No, I didn't get that impression."

"I see." I was determined to control my breathing. "What about the police?"

"What about the police?"

"Well, you must have mentioned him to them. Surely he's a suspect?"

"You *are* the amateur detective, aren't you. Yes, I mentioned him. But a first name with no surname isn't much to go on."

"I guess not," I said, calming down. "I never knew about him."

"Why should you?"

"No," I agreed, "why should I?"

"Anyway. Could be he's your missing link."

"Could be." I stood up, eager to get gone. "Anyway, you've been a great help. Thank you very much."

Marriner shrugged. "If you say so. I don't know that I have that much to contribute. It's always the same with dead people."

"How do you mean?"

"They turn into enigmas. I mean, they always were. But once they're dead we know they are," he said.

— X —

Soon after the evening at the Duke of Wellington there was a bank holiday and I went down to see my parents in Bognor Regis. They had only moved there after my father's retirement, so it had never been home as far as I was concerned, and I didn't visit them often. I have never quite understood the English compulsion to move to the seaside in one's twilight years. You take yourself off from all your familiar surroundings, from a location perfectly comfortable and convenient, and plant yourself in some godforsaken shithole full of bored holidaymakers and amusement arcades on the wind-lashed coast. What's more, with death coming ever closer, you sit staring at the biggest metaphor of nothingness Earth has to offer, the cold, endless and estranging sea. In this context, my dad's boat struck me as even more pathetic.

As always while at my parents' house, I reverted to impotent teenagerhood, sleeping late, consuming my mother's breakfast fry-ups, watching TV with a dull-eyed stare. When I took walks around the streets or along the seafront my mind felt empty, as if I had had my head removed. Perhaps it was the effect of the sea air. Everything I was and did in London seemed immeasurably distant and completely other. My mother was concerned about me, as usual. She worried that I was depressed, that I had no friends, that I might be going off the rails again. I tried not to get irritated with her, but her constant anxiety only made me anxious. It hardly indicated much confidence in my ability to make a life for myself.

"Really, Mother," I protested, "I can function, you know. I'm not a sociopath."

"Good gracious," said she (or words to that effect), "I never suggested that you were!" And then, inevitably, "I just worry that you should have someone to look after you."

"Mum, I'm never going to get married. I'm highly unlikely even to get a girlfriend. So you might as well get used to the idea and stop worrying."

"I don't see why you shouldn't ever have another girlfriend."

"Oh, don't you."

I stalked out of the kitchen, went upstairs and got on the internet.

Gladwell and I had not emailed each other since the previous week, and of course, he had no idea that I had sat in on his Wednesday night salon. No new parody had appeared on his blog lately, either. There was something exquisitely frustrating about this lack of fresh stimulus, akin to withdrawal from a drug of some kind, and with my mother's querulous queries ringing in my ears I felt an irresistible urge to communicate. I opened a blank email, typed in Gladwell as the recipient and sat with my fingers poised over the keyboard, desperately hunting for something intelligent to say.

Eventually I wrote:

> *Sorry I couldn't make it on Wednesday. Something came up (to coin a phrase).*
> *Any other challenges you'd like to set me?*

And I signed it:

Antinous

I fired it off without giving myself too much time to think, and then sat there stupidly waiting for a reply, but none came, of course. I stared out of the window, as if that would hurry things up. The conversation with my mother had rattled me. I did not particularly care to be reminded of that whole thing with Julie. It had been a mistake to visit my parents, but then, it always was. The resulting destabilisation generally took a couple of days to right itself and was a tremendous waste of time and energy. I couldn't very well abandon my mother entirely to my father's neglect, though, and I did feel a sense of filial duty toward both of them. They were, in a real way, all I had in the world, the only people who genuinely cared about me.

I returned downstairs and helped my mother with dinner preparations.

When I checked my email again a couple of hours later there was still nothing, and I began to feel a deep sinking sensation. I re-read my own message and winced. I shouldn't have signed it 'Antinous,' I shouldn't have made that stupid double entendre. What kind of idiot used the expression 'to coin a phrase' these days? It wasn't like I was ever going to put it up Gladwell or let him put it up me, so why make nudge-nudge wink-wink suggestions that I would? I was just desperate to connect, that was the truth of it, and I would use any kind of lie to make it happen.

I lay awake that night fantasising about what Gladwell might be doing with his bank holiday weekend. He was off at one of his toff friends' country estates, probably, picnicking on champagne with strawberries and cream (at this time I still believed his shtick about hailing from the upper classes), punting on the river (it wouldn't be pissing down with rain where he was) and haw-hawing over the camp antics of their acquaintances. Or he was back in London, holding court among a fascinating coterie of writers and artists, lounging around studios and galleries and having sex, lots of it, with beautiful young men (not that I was envious of that, of course). Wherever he was, I was sure he was not tucked up tight in his parents' tiny spare bedroom, trying to digest a stodgy meal of shepherd's pie followed by apple crumble and custard. He was not thinking about me.

Next morning I logged on at five a.m. and checked my email. My heart leapt. There was a message from Gladwell.

> *A challenge for Antinous? A number of ideas spring to mind, but I forbear. The gauntlet I lay down is G.G.*
> *G.*

A broad smile opened up across my face. I had read lots of Graham Greene. I'd been pretty much a fan at one time, in fact, though I'd cooled towards him over recent years. The perfect circumstances, all in all, from which to write a parody.

But I couldn't write it here. The atmosphere was too stultifying, the cloud of depression hung too dangerously close. I must get back to my flat in East Finchley as fast as possible.

At breakfast—which I gobbled down with indifference, rejecting the offered fry-up and settling for a single piece of toast—I felt rather than observed my mother's curious eyes upon me. My father, of course, never noticed anything, stuck behind his newspaper as usual. My mother said, "You seem in a very good mood this morning, Timmy!"

"I am in a very good mood. I'm in an exceptionally good mood."

"Any particular reason?"

The way she asked this, with those big, red-rimmed, anxiety-filled eyes, that edge of suspicion and uncertainty to her voice, drove me wild with irritation. I was more sure than ever that I could do no writing here, that I must return to London without delay. I pushed back my chair and got up from the table, slurping a mouthful of tea and leaving the rest.

"I have to go," I announced. Even my father looked up.

"Go? Go where?"

"Back to London. I have to leave right away."

"But you were going to stay till Monday!"

"Well, now I can't. I have work to do."

"Can't you do it here?"

"No, I can't. I have to go home to do it. Understand what I mean? Home. My home. The place where I live my life." I was being unnecessarily brutal, I knew, but for some reason I was unable to stop myself. My mother began to cry.

"Don't speak like that to your mother, Timothy," my father said.

"I'm sorry. But I have to leave. That's all."

I fled upstairs to my room and began stuffing things haphazardly into my overnight bag. Much to my annoyance, my mother followed.

"What's the matter?" she demanded tearfully. "What's happened?"

"Nothing. Something's come up, that's all."

"We hardly ever see you."

"I know, I know. It's just—work is crazy, we have to run all the time just to stand still."

"I worry about you."

"Please don't!" I gave my clothes an extra hard shove, and pulled the zip closed viciously.

"You seem so up and down. Are you seeing a doctor regularly?"

"I don't need to see a bloody doctor!" I exploded. The violence of the explosion alarmed even me. I wasn't doing my case any favours, I knew, so I got a grip on myself and said, more gently, "Honestly, Mum, I'm fine. I'm just overworked. And I need to get back and sort this problem out."

"All right." She reached out and put her arms around me. "I wish you would come and stay for longer some time, though. Take a proper holiday. The sea air would do you good."

"I'll do that. Thanks." We hugged. I felt a sudden wave of tenderness pass through me, a sudden sense of compunction. "I love you, Mum."

"I love you, Timmy."

I released myself. I got out of the house and on the train back to London as fast as I could.

— XI —

After my visit to Ray Marriner I hesitated where to turn next. The exposure of my alias had left me thoroughly rattled, and for several days I was quite paranoid, expecting the police to knock on my door at any moment. Media coverage of the murder had dropped off completely, and I could only assume the investigation had run into a sandbank. But there was no way of knowing for sure. Who could tell what far-fetched leads they might be following behind the scenes? Above all, I didn't want to get caught up in the inquiry. That would hamper my quest no end.

Soon enough, however, I began to calm down. The fact of the matter was, my alias had not been exposed; Ray could hardly have mentioned the name Timothy so casually if it had. As he himself had observed, a first name with no surname wasn't a lot to go on. Still, I cursed myself for having let my defences down so unnecessarily. It was pure ego that had led me to reveal my identity—half of it, at any rate—to Gladwell. I had been lured by his charm, his blandishments, and my own foolish desire to be known for who I really was.

I wondered who else he might have mentioned me to. Almost anyone was a possibility. He didn't know the meaning of the word discretion. In any case, there was no point in trying to second-guess the issue. I decided to carry on as if the name Timothy had nothing to do with me. That was the best way of ensuring no-one else made the connection.

I chose to get in touch with Anwar Mussa next, if only because I was convinced he was the least savvy of Gladwell's inner circle. He at least could be relied on not to start putting two and two together or making five. I expected to be able to run rings around him, and if he had any manuscripts in his keeping, I felt pretty sure of managing to lay hands on them.

Mussa was working as a barista at a coffee shop in Islington to help fund his masters degree. He asked me to meet him there at the end of his shift. I arrived about fifteen minutes early, made myself known and sat down with a glass of cold milk in one corner of the steamy and frankly rather unpleasant-smelling café to watch him at work. He wore a black apron over a pinstriped shirt with a small black hat perched on the crown of his head. On almost anyone else it would have looked ridiculous but in the case of Mussa it only enhanced his strangely innocent beauty. I could not help but admire his expertise with the various machines. He moved from one to another with the grace of a skilled technician.

When his shift ended he disappeared into the back for a few minutes and emerged in a t-shirt with a small rucksack over his shoulder. He had been transformed back into an ordinary student. He pulled out the chair opposite and set his bag down on the floor at his feet.

"Actually," I said, "do you mind if we go somewhere else? No offence, but I don't really care for the smell of coffee. And that machine is kind of noisy."

He shrugged, and stood up again. He was quite tall. "Sure. Whatever you like." We left the place and stepped out into the baking late afternoon sunshine.

London was at its grittiest and most oppressive, and the rush-hour traffic was belching out fumes far viler than those in the café. We set off up the street, walking fast although I had no idea where we were headed. I had hoped to find some quieter and more private venue, but nothing suitable presented itself; only grim-looking wine bars and franchises heaving with tourists and office workers.

"Let's keep going," Mussa said. "I know a place."

He turned off abruptly down a set of steps that led to the canal. Sudden tranquillity greeted us. Even the air seemed fresher. There were trees, water, ducks and hardly any people. We sat down on the first empty bench we came to.

"Will this do?" Mussa asked.

"This is great," I said. "This is perfect."

"I come here to read sometimes, before and after my shift. It's a refuge." I glanced at him warily. His tallness made me self-conscious. "So," he continued, "you're writing a thesis on Ralph?"

"That's right. My doctorate. For Oxford University."

"You look somehow familiar. Were you a friend of his?"

"Not really. I used to sit in on his soirées now and again."

"I see. So are you exploring parody in general, or just focussing on Ralph?"

"Uh—well, you know." His pure eyes were fixed on me unnervingly; his lashes were long and girlish. "Gladwell mainly. Of course, parody will be a large part of it." Not parody of Ralph, of course. Not parody of Ralph.

"He was brilliant," Mussa said. "He was a genius."

"Maybe."

"Definitely. I've never known anyone like him." He stared at the water. "I still can't believe he's dead."

"No, it's hard to take in."

"I came here with him a couple of times. We sat on this very bench."

"Really?"

"He taught me so much. He got me into reading all these great old authors—Voltaire, Rousseau, Swift—and he helped me see through all the crap, you know? All the junk we were being spoon-fed with at college. And he made me laugh. More than anything he made me laugh."

"He was certainly an original."

Mussa gazed out across the canal, where the ducks were gathering noisily, no doubt expecting breadcrumbs. Despite his height he had a fugitive, tremulous presence. "He knew he'd be killed. He told me on several occasions."

I shivered in the sunshine.

"I didn't believe him. If only I had."

"Who did he think wanted to kill him?"

"He wouldn't say. He just said he knew it would happen one day. Like a premonition."

"Did you mention this to the police?"

"Are you kidding? I didn't have anything to do with the police."

"How come?"

He looked at me as though I were insane. "I'm from a good Muslim family. If they found out about me we'd be ruined." He began tugging at the leather bracelet around his wrist. "That's what's made this whole thing all the harder."

"I see."

"I mean, I knew we were never going to be a couple. But I loved him. I really loved him."

I felt quite sorry for the poor boy. He seemed a gentle soul. It struck me that Gladwell had tended to go for this type—soft and vulnerable, younger than himself, easily moulded. Only in my case had he seriously miscalculated. Or had he?

"I never understood why he fell for *that man*," Mussa went on.

"You mean Aaron Milner?"

"I could tell he was just a user. Right from the start. But I don't know. Maybe Ralph liked to be used."

I refrained from comment.

"This whole big wedding and everything... I didn't understand it. I guess Ralph was head over heels. But I knew it wouldn't last." He looked up at me, as if seeking justification. "Less than a year, that's all. I didn't need any wedding. I would have loved him forever."

I remained silent, uncomfortable with his intensity. Mussa went on, "I wouldn't be surprised if he were the murderer."

"Who—Aaron?"

"*That man.*"

"He isn't, you know. He has a solid alibi."

"I don't care if he has an alibi. I think he did it."

"Well, theories apart, my interest is in Gladwell's work rather than his death."

"Of course. I'm sorry. I'd be very happy to discuss Ralph's work with you. It's what he would want most, for that to take precedence."

"Absolutely. And I'm sure we could discuss him—his work, I mean—till the cows come home. But at the moment my chief interest lies in his unpublished writings."

"How do you mean—unpublished?"

"Material that has not appeared in any public forum, either in print or on the internet."

The possible existence of such material seemed to strike him as bizarre, in this age where to write was to publish. "Such as?"

"Well, rumour has it that he produced a number of novels."

"*Novels?*" For the first time, this utterly serious boy showed signs of amusement. "Ralph would never have written any novels."

"No?"

"Absolutely not. He didn't need to. He didn't have that *deeply commonplace* urge." I heard Gladwell's words speaking through the young man's voice. "It's one of the things that made him exceptional."

"Is it, indeed?" I smiled.

"Yes. In an age where practically everyone is writing novels, the novel has become a bankrupt form. The parodist is the scourge of the novelist." He was directly echoing his mentor now, except that I seemed to recall Gladwell saying "the righteous scourge."

"Nicely quoted," I replied. "I don't suppose it has occurred to you that Gladwell was young once, and that he too had a journey to take in order to reach his eventual… *lofty* position?"

Mussa stared at me, blinking.

"How could anyone be as bitter as that about fiction," I went on, "unless they had once written it themselves?"

"No. No way."

"It's basic psychology. The failed novelist is the scourge of the successful one."

"That's a lie. It's you that's bitter."

"Not in the least. I have nothing to be bitter about. *I* have never written any novels."

"You envy him. You want to tear him down." Mussa rose from his seat. He towered over me, his face aquiver.

"I don't know what you're getting so worked up about. Please—sit down." Mussa sat. He was quite biddable. "The motivation for his work doesn't in any way detract from the power of it. On the contrary. The bitterer the parodist, the sharper his parody."

"Maybe..." The boy sat with head hanging, the very picture of despondency and grief. "Ralph loved literature."

"No doubt. And that's the paradox that drove his writing."

"Maybe you're right," he murmured.

"So you see, I'm not looking to tear him down. Just do him justice."

Mussa dashed away more tears with his forearm. I had never met a man who cried so easily. "I just can't bear to think of him being attacked."

"I always thought he rather relished it."

"But now he can't retaliate. And when they... When he was murdered, he couldn't retaliate."

He had a point.

"They stabbed him in the back," Anwar Mussa said.

"I know."

"*In the back*. The bastards. What kind of a coward does that?"

I didn't reply at first. I didn't care to speculate on what kind of coward. It had always struck me as a peculiarly appropriate style of death. "Aaron Milner?" I said eventually.

He shook his head. "I don't really believe that it was Aaron. I think it was a conspiracy of some kind. The literary establishment. They hired a hit man to get rid of him."

"Do you think that would really be in their interest?"

"I don't know. I don't know. Then why?" he demanded passionately. "Why?"

I turned cold to my bones. In a strange way, it was as though I was feeling the reality of Gladwell's murder for the first time. Even my meeting with his mother had not affected me like this.

"We may never find out."

"We will," he said, through gritted teeth. "We will!"

I reflected that if the police felt one tenth of his passion, their investigations would have advanced more quickly. But that wasn't my main concern right now. "So you really can't help me?"

"What with?"

"His novels."

Mussa shook his head. "I'm sorry. He never showed me anything like that."

I sighed. Of all the people I had spoken to, he was the first I believed to have told me the whole truth.

— XII —

I still recalled the occasion on which Gladwell had made his pronouncements about the modern novel. It was at one of his salons in the Duke of Wellington, some time after the commencement of our "collaboration." I put the word in quotation marks for reasons I shall soon make perfectly clear. We had already got well and truly into the swing of things, although so far as Gladwell was aware we had never met face to face. By now my nickname of Antinous had become so firmly entrenched I would have been thoroughly mortified were he to see the real, frog-ugly countenance of Jim Tate. But I thrilled to the awareness that my knowledge of Gladwell, his comings and goings, the intimacies of his private life, kept growing and growing.

As soon as I got back to London from my parents' house I had set to work on my parody of Graham Greene. In fact, my mind had been buzzing the whole way on the train and despite the fact that I can't type on trains because it gives me travel sickness, I had practically the whole thing written in my head by the time I sat down at the computer. There was a deliciously Eeyore tone to Greene's writing which I lunged into like a panther attacking fresh meat. All that Fall of Man tragedy and world-weariness was so ripe for send-up, I ripped through it almost effortlessly. And of course, he had his tics of style like any other writer, even the greatest. As I wrote, occasionally laughing out loud, I realised that I had never felt pleasure like this while working on my novel. It occurred to me that where the writer receives no pleasure from his writing the reader can surely derive none from reading it.

I emailed it off to Gladwell and fell into a fevered sleep. In my dream, I was standing outside his house in Tufnell Park; it was night, but the moon was shining so brightly it was like day. I mounted the steps to the front door and rang the bell. As I did so, I was aware that I was breaking cover and was alarmed at my own actions, but another, inner part of me was perfectly calm. Gladwell opened the door and was delighted to see me. I felt a great warmth towards him, as though we had been friends for years and this meeting were the fulfilment of all my longing. Even as I dreamt, and was aware that I dreamt, I had to acknowledge there was a certain truth in this. I *did* want to reveal myself to Gladwell and be embraced by him as he was embracing me now. He led me upstairs to a room impossibly warm and inviting, with damask wallpaper and deep soft armchairs and sofa; a fire was burning brightly in the grate. A bottle of wine and two glasses stood on the table, as though my host had been expecting me. We clinked glasses and Gladwell, with the most loving of expressions, drew near, embraced me once more and we began to kiss…

At this point I woke abruptly, wiping my lips. I was horrified. My waking self did not find Ralph Gladwell even remotely attractive. The idea of kissing him made me nauseous. At the same time, the undeniable pleasure I had felt in my dream tugged at the edges of my consciousness. I reached for the glass of water at my bedside and gulped it down. Then in an effort to sweep the disturbing impression from my mind I sat down at my computer. A fresh email from Gladwell awaited me there.

He was, as always, sparing with his praise, but I could tell that he liked my parody of Greene. We were on the same wavelength; he had laughed, but he had also appreciated the more forensic aspects of my dissection. He had never much cared for Greene himself, he admitted; he found him too moralistic, or rather, he had that strange combination of moralism and nihilism, often found in religious people, which made them responsible for so many acts of massacre.

I awaited what I now suspected to be the inevitable upshot, and sure enough, it came. A week or two later I opened Gladwell's blog to find my Greene parody—tweaked a little here and there, but essentially the same—gracing the home page. I had to admit, it gave me a thrill to see it there. For the first time in my life, a ready-made audience of admiring readers was mine. And something about inhabiting Gladwell's persona in this way was more gratifying than if my own dull name had graced the byline. The blind fury I had felt over Katherine Mansfield did not manifest itself this time. I only wanted to continue what I had started.

I sat for a long time composing my next email. Finally I wrote:

> *Nice parody of Greene in your last posting.*
> *Who shall we do next?*
> *Antinous*

At this point I didn't know for sure where I was taking things; I only knew I needed to stay in the game.

As for Gladwell, he can have been under no illusions, because he wrote back shortly after:

How about Papa?

I was surprised at his picking such an easy target as Hemingway, but perhaps he was running out of ideas. And maybe that was the point. Gladwell was running out of juice, I thought: he was coming to the end of his inspiration. If that was the case, my advent in his life was fortuitous.

As I was later to discover, it was not quite as simple as that, but I will not pre-empt myself. I tossed off the Hemingway parody without breaking a sweat, sent it along to Gladwell, and we were on our way. I became his ghostwriter.

Mansfield, Greene, Hemingway; Amis, Updike, Roth; no-one escaped our ambit, or survived the lethal nib of my metaphorical pen. Byatt, Mantel, Ishiguro; Austen, Bowen, Poe; writers old and new were decapitated by our gleaming scythe. I did the young lion's share of the composition, while Gladwell, the ailing lion (as I came to regard him), sharpened a point here and there or erased a weaker sentence, but rarely came up with a joke of his own any more and even, as time passed, allowed me to suggest our next victim, as if he didn't know whom to choose or, I sometimes suspected, had lost his taste for the kill.

Throughout all this we never acknowledged openly what we were doing, or engaged in much dialogue beyond what was necessary to our project. I knew it and he knew it; that was enough. As we grew more familiar, he began to address little tendernesses toward me: that I was 'Antinous' was our joke at first, but he named me occasionally his 'sweet Antinous,' or his 'deadly Antinous' (referring solely to my abilities as a parodist, I hasten to add) and even signed himself, affectionately, as 'G x.' And I found that I enjoyed these endearments, rendered harmless as they were by the medium of email, in a way I should certainly not have done had they been offered in person. As for me, I relished playing hard to get, though I could not resist baiting him with some provocative word or image from time to time, especially when his own expressions of warmth grew ominously absent.

It was around this time that he was becoming involved with Aaron Milner, a fledgling of that upper-crust public-school set he sometimes flirted with, much to his friends' disgust. Milner had a reputation as a bit of a man-killer, and Gladwell was not the first father figure with whom he had been linked. All Gladwell's true friends, so far as I could tell, were dismayed by his infatuation and warned him against it. They rightly thought he was making a fool of himself. Of course, he was head over heels and took not the slightest bit of notice.

The night of the tirade against the modern novel was one of the rare occasions when Milner himself was present. Aaron made no secret of the fact that he hated the Duke of Wellington and despised the group who met there: the lit'ry-farty set he, without much poetry, called them. And he did seem very out of place among them: tall, golden, beautiful, in his finely-striped Savile Row shirt and with a bored look on his face, he was clearly superior to the old college friends, geeks and acolytes who populated Gladwell's salon. The trouble was, he showed no loyalty to Gladwell either, checking his phone while he was holding forth, or getting up in the middle of his impromptu lectures to order fresh drinks or step outside for one of his frequent cigarettes.

It was painful to watch, especially for me, knowing as I did the secret decline in Gladwell's creative powers. One saw him being humiliated and taking it, like a doting fool. Flickers of embarrassment ran over the faces of his friends, a number of them visibly winced, but the Parodist did not seem to notice. He went on speaking regardless of the fact that everyone was distracted and no-one was really listening.

I don't recall exactly what set him off that night. Maybe it was some inchoate sense that he was being undermined, maybe it was growing frustration with his writer's block. Perhaps he was simply drunk. Either way, before one knew what was up he had launched into a demolition of contemporary novelists notable for its venom, its bitterness and—unusually until then— its bad temper.

"The novel once meant something," he was saying, "but in this day and age where everyone is writing novels, it has become a bankrupt form. All these novels are like microbes swarming on the rotting corpse of literature. Not the novel as entertainment, I've nothing against that, though that is hardly worth talking about. I mean the *worthy* novel, the *serious* novel, the novel as a *work of art*. Pah! Nothing sticks in my craw more, and that includes the *poetry* and *history* and *philosophy* and all those other bastardised forms that pass for culture nowadays. In fact, don't get me started on the word *culture*!" He took a large swallow of beer, and nearly choked; a dribble of foam ran down his chin, and like an old man he failed to notice it. "It wants purging, all those who peddle it should be taken out and shot, but failing that, they want the shit ripped out of them unmercifully. And the novelists most of all. The parodist is the righteous scourge of the novelist. In fact, the parodist should be carried on the shoulders of the people with garlands of laurel round his noble brow."

At this point Milner got up, apparently oblivious, and pulled his cigarette packet from his breast pocket. Gladwell smiled up at him and continued, "The moment the novel as entertainment split off from the novel as work of art the form was doomed, not only as art but also as entertainment, because art that does not amuse is essentially lifeless, and besides, there are so many easier and better ways of being entertained these days. The contemporary novelist can't get that split out of his mind; the more he tries not to think of it, the more he thinks of it, and the less able he is to create anything worth sod all as art or pleasure." Milner edged his way past Collins, Mussa, Marriner, and made for the top of the stairs, a cigarette already in his mouth and his lighter in his hand, the expensive engraved lighter Ralph had given him for his thirtieth birthday and that he would later take back and keep as a memento of his ex-husband, even though he didn't smoke.

Gladwell was in full flow now; he didn't break stride as Milner made off indifferently downstairs. "So, in the eighties you got the *Marks and Spencer* school of fiction, full of elaborate descriptions of fine dining and broderie anglais nightgowns and expensive bathroom furniture, appropriately for that decade of conspicious consumption," (I doubt whether anyone knew precisely which novelist he had in mind, but his references did raise a knowing smile or two) "and heading into the nineties you got the *exotic historical* school of fiction as everyone climbed on the post-colonial bandwagon, we all needed educating you see, and what pleasanter means of educating ourselves than through a nice novel? I sometimes call this the *bougainvillea school*. Then you got the contemporary version of the working class novel, we'll call that the *fuckshite* novel, and the *reference library* novel that tells you all about diamond-cutting or sheep diseases or sewerage treatment while the protagonist goes through their *personal voyage of discovery*. And let's not forget all those faux-intellectual novels with titles like *Shakespeare's Teapot* or *Proust's Snotrag* or *Kafka's Underpants*. But they're quite out of fashion now, or at least I hope they are. No, since the dawn of the new century it's all about the world situation, how tedious, we now have the *terrorism school* and the *bank-crash school* and the, oh my God, the *dystopian school*, all of which we can wrap up under the title *relevant school* because nothing justifies a work of art more thoroughly right now than being relevant. The more relevant it is the more hope it has of justifying its existence and the less chance it has of ever being art, but in the rush to justify themselves the modern novelists are like a bunch of lemmings jumping off a cliff, which quite frankly I wish they would, because nothing ever had less reason to exist than they do."

Someone said, "But then you would have nothing left to satirise."

"If I had nothing left to satirise I could live a life of ease under a clear blue sky, eat my portion blamelessly and tend my vine. But sadly, that will never be the case." Gladwell leaned back in his seat, arms akimbo, looking every inch the world-weary patriarch he claimed to be. "It's my fate to be the tireless scourge of all this *dreck*, though I get very little thanks for it and less and less satisfaction. And the only pay I ever receive is laughter."

Ever loyal, his audience duly laughed. And yet there was a vulnerability he conveyed tonight, through his tone or his face or his body language, as though he had become stretched out thin somehow, transparent, and we could see right through him to the tangle of rage and resentment that lay beneath.

I have to admit I felt sorry for him that evening, sitting off to the side discreetly drinking my orange juice. Now that I look back on it, I see that it was the beginning of the end. His coming under Milner's thrall marked a change for the worse in all his relationships, including that with himself. Though his true friends remained faithful, something of pity now tinged their attitude. Doubtless he felt this, which would explain why he eventually turned so foul towards them. By the time of his death, in fact, it is probably true to say he was on good terms with nobody. And when I look back now I cannot help but wonder: did he really mean to provoke someone to kill him? And out of all of us, might he have chosen me?

"If it were up to me I would forbid the writing of novels from now on," he continued, oblivious to his listeners' growing discomfort. "Not only that, but I would order bonfires. Look at your shocked little faces! He's a Nazi! But, believe me, it's the only way to get the value of the novel back. Let there be great bonfires of all the candy-coloured dreck and all the throwaway titles and all the earnest dross poetically written, yes and the fuckshite literature antipoetically written. Let it be kindled with Kindles—never was a thing more aptly named! And then let there be a moratorium of fifty years. And when we're starved and lean and desperate and pure—maybe then we will be ready for new novels. Maybe then we'll be in need of them."

It was Gladwell's apologia: the fullest statement I ever heard him make. And he was quite right, of course. But nobody wanted to hear him that evening, and the person he was really trying to reach, the person who was generating his anger—Aaron Milner—was not there at all. He was standing outside in the square, smoking his cigarette, and no doubt flirting with someone younger and more beautiful.

— XIII —

AFTER ANWAR MUSSA, MY next target was Rob Collins at the university. I was rather wary of meeting him, because I knew it would be hard to pull the wool over his eyes. He was not an artist in any sense of the word, he had his feet firmly planted on the ground and of all Ralph's friends he was the least bedazzled. On the upside, I was more likely to get sense out of him than any of the others.

We met in his office at the end of the working day; it was only a couple of tube stops from my own place of employment. It felt strange to walk the corridors Gladwell himself had frequented for so many years. I tried to imagine him there, but it was almost impossible. The building was one of those cheap glass ones thrown up in the seventies, ugly in the extreme, hot as a greenhouse and just as characterless. Décor-wise, the theme was bluebottle green. No ghosts could haunt it. It was a sick building.

Collins met me in the entrance foyer, shook my hand with the firm grip of a rugby player and grabbed two coffees from the machine before marching me up to his cubbyhole on the second floor. It was the summer holidays and there were no students about. Sharp late-afternoon shards of sunlight fell through the large plate-glass windows of the corridor, nearly roasting us alive. But his tiny office had no windows.

It was stuffed to the ceiling with shelves of textbooks, bulging manila files, ring-binders and untidy piles of foolscap. More piles stood on the floor, so that there was barely room for the desk and two chairs. The desk itself was completely covered with books and documents, as well as a computer which looked heavily used.

"Sorry about the conditions," Collins cheerfully apologised. "You should see where they put the junior lecturers."

"Not at all," I smiled. "Feels just like home."

"Actually," he announced, leaning back in his office chair with his big legs crossed and his coffee cup in his hands, "I've been expecting you."

"You have?"

"Oh, yes. We're a tight-knit little community, you know, we friends of Ralph. Word gets around."

"I guess it does." I hesitated. "What did they tell you about me?"

"Frankly? That you're a tight-arsed queer who's probably never been fucked and talks like an undergraduate essay on the Edwardian novel. Except that you talk about Ralph. With whom you claim to have collaborated, though that must be a total lie."

I don't know if I blenched, but I felt my jaw tighten. "Anything else? Please don't hold back."

"They also said you were an ugly little troll, since you insist on knowing." He paused as though waiting, then smiled and added, "But since you haven't already left the room, I have to believe the rest of what they told me, which is that you're very determined to get hold of what you want."

"And what is that, exactly?"

He smiled, sipping his coffee. "Why don't you explain?"

"What's the point? You already know everything. Far be it from me to steal your thunder."

"All right. You're after these unpublished novels Ralph may or may not have written. What I want to know is why?"

"He did write them."

"Be that as it may. What do you want with them?"

"I'm curious."

"Curious?"

"I admire his work and I want to know what kind of a novelist he was."

Collins gazed at me fixedly, cradling his coffee cup. His dark, craglike face was full of scepticism.

I steadied myself and explained, "I'm writing a study. I'm sure they told you that."

He only gave a short bark of a laugh. "Ha!" Then he leaned forward and put down his cup. There was barely room for it among the books and papers.

"What else could I possibly be interested in them for?"

"I don't know. That's what I'm trying to find out."

"You seem very suspicious."

"Maybe because you're such a suspicious character."

"Am I?"

"To me, yes. Maybe the others didn't see it. But I do. Poor old Ralph is hardly cold in his grave. You pursue his mother, you pursue his friends, you tell lies about being his collaborator. About writing some book. Everything about you is off. Who the hell are you?"

"Look," I said, rising. "Clearly this isn't going anywhere. I might as well get out of your way."

"And now you want to leave. It's odd, that."

"Hardly. You've done nothing but insult me from the moment we started. It's amazing I've stayed this long."

"Isn't it just?" I was beginning to hate this man. His black bushy eyebrows, his broad rugby-playing shoulders, his blank, hardman expression: they all spelled danger I should have seen coming. "Sit down," he commanded. I sat.

He stood up in turn and began moving about the cramped little room, ostensibly consulting various books and files. I followed him with my eyes, wondering what he would come up with next. He wanted to give the impression he was a step ahead of me. I doubted it.

"If you know so much about Ralph and his work, then you'll have a fair idea what he thought of novelists," Collins said. "Basically, he thought they were a bunch of wankers."

"Maybe it takes one to know one."

"Is that your angle? Gladwell was a wanker? Hardly very reverential."

"I don't intend to be reverential."

"Good. Ralph doesn't deserve it."

"I think he was a very complex person. Part wanker, part..."

"Please don't say genius. Please, for God's sake, don't say genius. Or I really will throw you out of the room."

"I was going to say crusader."

"He was that. Tediously so."

"You didn't respect him much."

"I'd known him too long to respect him." He reflected, adding, "I respected him as much as he deserved." I let the silence hang awhile; I was reluctant to hand him any more ammunition. "He wasn't as complex as all that," Collins said, after some further thought.

"Oh?"

He looked me in the eye, and for a fraction of a second I could see inside him. There really was someone messed up and dangerous in there. "Bluntly: he was your basic narcissist. Your basic failure." He laughed, as though I had challenged him. "Oh-ho, you don't think Ralph was a failure? He was the Parodist, the great satirist, everybody worshipped at his altar? He thought he was a failure and I thought he was a failure."

"Yes, I know," I replied calmly.

"What do you mean, you know? What do you know about it?"

"I know. I was his ghostwriter for two years. I think that gives me a certain degree of insight."

Collins seemed genuinely lost for words. He stopped his futile wanderings and stared at me fixedly for several seconds. Then he flexed his powerful shoulders. "Ralph didn't need a ghostwriter."

"He did, actually. Towards the end he was totally burned out. He'd lost the wherewithal to write anything."

"What rubbish."

"I don't expect you to believe me. It's the truth, however."

Collins leaned on the desk with both knuckles; it gave him a remarkably simian appearance. Then he sat down, expelling a large sigh. "If that's really the case, then things were even worse than I thought." He rubbed his lips with his forefinger. "Poor Ralph."

"You're still capable of feeling sorry for him, then."

"I've done nothing but feel sorry for him, ever since…" He seemed about to confess to what I was sure was their long-ago affair, but instead he did so in a more indirect manner. "Since he took up with Milner, who was totally wrong for him. I told him so. But he wouldn't take any notice."

"No—well, he wasn't the most persuadable of people."

"Obstinate as a mule. Especially if it would get him into trouble. He went his own way, did Ralph. That's why I can't see him putting his name to anyone else's work, for example."

"My theory is that he was in a kind of denial."

"How so?"

"He took my work, changed a word or a phrase here and there and believed he'd written it, effectively."

"He'd have to be pretty far gone to believe that."

My silence spoke for itself.

"Poor Ralph," Collins said again. Then he fixed me once more with his laser eye. "But what was in it for you?"

"It was good experience for me. I was honing my skills."

He shook his head. "No, I don't buy that."

"All right. I liked seeing his name on my work. It gave me a kick."

"It gave you a kick, having that power over him."

"Yes, it did. But I was never inclined to use it."

"What a saint."

"I'm very far from a saint. It just never occurred to me."

"You never asked him for money?"

"Of course not."

"Humph!"

"I liked having that relationship with him." The moment these words escaped me, I wished them unsaid.

"Because you don't do the *sex thing*!" Collins guffawed.

"I found it intellectually challenging," I said quietly.

Collins studied me for some time. It was hard to tell

what he was thinking. "Anyway," he said at last, "none of this means he would have wanted you to have access to his private papers."

"He might have done."

"Then it's a shame he didn't appoint a literary executor."

"I don't suppose he expected to die."

Collins glared at me. "Didn't he?"

My heart began pounding furiously.

"Actually, Ralph always said someone would murder him one day," Collins went on. "I assumed it was rhetoric."

"It probably was."

"Creepy, though. Don't you find it creepy?"

I didn't know how to answer. He kept staring at me.

"When did you see him last?" he asked, with faked casualness.

"I don't remember precisely. Why do you ask?"

"Just curious."

"We didn't meet very often. We didn't need to."

"No, I don't suppose you did. Still, it's the sort of thing you'd remember, isn't it? The last time you see somebody who gets murdered."

"I think it was a couple of weeks before."

"At his place?"

"No. At a pub in Camden."

"Ralph never went to any pubs in Camden."

"That's why we used to meet there. He didn't want to bump into anyone he knew."

"Interesting. I thought you said he was in denial."

"It was complicated." I was saying too much, but it was all running on so fast. I passed a hand across my forehead. I was burning up.

Suddenly, Collins seemed inclined to let me off the

hook. He placed his huge, meaty paws flat on the desk in front of him and contemplated them for a few seconds. Then he picked up a pen and scribbled something. "Listen, I don't know if I can help you with these manuscripts you're looking for and I'm not sure if I want to. But I'll ask around and see what I can find out. Why don't you let me have your number?"

"You have my email address."

"Yes, I do. But your number would come in handy."

"All right." I pulled out my mobile reluctantly and read off my number. He copied it down. As he did so I was filled with a hollow sense of foreboding.

Collins smiled at me, a broad, false smile. "Look, I'm sorry I've been so rude. I'm a bit of a vulgar lout, as my students will tell you."

"No problem."

"I'm sure you're a harmless chap. You certainly look it. But we're all a bit jumpy these days, given—what happened."

I nodded. He sat smiling at me fixedly.

"I can't help wondering," he continued. "With an ability like yours, didn't you ever want to produce something of your own?"

"How do you mean?"

"I mean, write something original—under your own name?"

"I'm not good enough." He was trying to adopt a sympathetic expression, but his features continued to express suspicion. "A man has to realise his limitations."

He grimaced. "You remind me of Ralph. He used to talk like that. It made me sad." He added, "Everything about Ralph makes me sad these days."

It was all I could take. I rose dizzily to my feet and got the hell out of there.

— XIV —

FOR QUITE SOME TIME, while Gladwell and Milner were in the first full flush of their relationship, while the wedding preparations went ahead and the marriage took place (a big, ritzy affair, with lilies and a silver marquee and a live jazz band) and then during the honeymoon on Barbados and the honeymoon period after, he and I had very little contact. I sent parodies and they appeared on his website without even the token changes Gladwell had previously felt obliged to make. Then they failed to appear as he neglected the blog, and something of a backlog began to build. I appreciated that he was busy with his personal life, but began to feel increasingly frustrated. I realised that even though my work was not appearing under my own name, or even *because* it was appearing under Gladwell's, I had come to need the thrill of seeing it online the way addicts need their fix. His failure to post it left me irritable and restless.

Something else started to dawn on me in those days: the degree to which I was addicted to my correspondence with Gladwell. If he did not respond to my emails within the day, I began to think he had completely abandoned me. I imagined storming round to his house (where he was unlikely to be, in fact, gadding about as he did at all hours with Milner) and confronting him, or at least firing off hysterical and demanding messages. I was his collaborator, after all, I was the one who was closest to him in everything that was most important. Milner of the low intellectual wattage could not begin to compete with me in that department. Pretty he might be, but I alone could communicate with Gladwell's mind and soul.

Fortunately I managed to contain myself, and resisted the temptation to send those emails. Once again I succeeded in biding my time. I knew the Milner scenario could not last, that the honeymoon period would end sooner or later and when it did, there I would still be, patient and faithful, waiting to provide the Parodist with the sustenance he needed.

Sometimes I would get off the tube a few stops early on my way home from work and linger for a short while outside Gladwell's house, which had a To Let sign posted in front of it. I even inquired of the letting agency and arranged to view the property. It was still part-furnished, and I derived a certain dank thrill from seeing Gladwell's household belongings, but the soul of the place was missing and the experience only left me more agitated, like a brief relapse while trying to go cold turkey. Gladwell was living with Milner at his mansion flat. I hung around on the pavement opposite the ornate building, looking up at the windows with their gauzy curtains and wondering how he could stand to be holed up in there with such a shallow, selfish partner.

The worst of it was, Gladwell stopped coming to the Wednesday night salons, no doubt on the urging of his new husband, who would have told him what a bore they were. Without him, predictably, the gatherings fell apart. I began to find myself turning up there alone and sitting stupidly in my regular corner listening to nothing and observing no-one. After the third such occasion I realised it was all over and made my way home with a feeling of emptiness I can hardly describe.

Lavish parties were taking place at the mansion flat, but to these, of course, I was not invited. I began to wonder whether I had played my cards right. If I had made myself known to Gladwell I might have been part of the inner circle by now. I could be one of the shadows moving about behind those lighted windows, laughing and talking, impressing the company with my native wit. Except I knew, in my heart, that that was not how it would be; Milner would never allow someone like me across his threshold, and I had no native wit, I was not a talker. It was better this way, I reflected as I took my lonely walk back to the tube station. My relationship with Gladwell remained something secret and apart, unique, different from these superficial encounters he was now enjoying.

Then came the first sign of trouble to give me hope. One night as I was loitering across the road from the flat (there was a Starbucks nearby, and I would warm myself with the occasional hot chocolate before returning to my accustomed spot) who should come storming out of the front entrance but Aaron Milner himself, very obviously in a flaming temper. He was dressed in light chinos and a shiny grey shirt, and was coatless despite the cold. By the looks of things he had fled abruptly in the midst of some argument.

For a second or two he remained hovering from foot to foot, apparently at a loss where to go next. It was still early evening, and people and traffic passed by in a regular stream. I knew I could remain unobtrusive, and moved slightly closer in order to observe what would transpire. Before long, as I had anticipated, Gladwell himself emerged. He appeared a little older, a little less authoritative to my eyes, but then, I had not seen him in several weeks.

He hesitated a moment, looking right and left, spotted Aaron and immediately approached and laid a conciliatory hand upon his arm. Milner flung him off. He tried again. The brat lashed out, swore viciously, and dashing across the road without a care for the traffic, barrelled straight into me.

"Get out of the way, you ugly balding git!"

He fled off down the street, leaving me winded and Gladwell in an apparent state of shock.

Insulted as I was, I could not help feeling gratified by this incident. It demonstrated beyond doubt that all was not well in paradise, and though I experienced a small pang on Ralph's behalf as he stood there mournfully gazing after his vanished love, I inwardly rejoiced to think that this farce might soon be over. After lingering like an abandoned dog on the pavement for a minute or two, he returned indoors disconsolate, and I walked briskly to Starbucks with a smile on my lips.

I decided to make hay, and as soon as I had my hot chocolate sat down to write to him. It was essential that I reach him before Milner's return and the inevitable reconciliation that would leave them feeling, for the time being at least, even closer than before. I may never have been in a proper relationship myself, but I knew enough about human nature to realise the aphrodisiac power of a good quarrel. I decided to keep it simple.

> *Doing OK?*
> *Antinous*

The reply came almost immediately.

> *Shitty shitty shitty. Make me laugh, sweet Antinous.*

I did not try to suppress the broad grin breaking across my face.

> *Let us go, then, you and I,* I wrote back
> *When the mood cloacal is spread out against the sky*
> *Like a great intestine burst upon a table*

And Gladwell, also smiling, I imagine, responded:

> *Let us go, through certain rat-infested sewers,*
> *The haunts of literary reviewers*

And I:

> *Of hungry parodists rifling through bins*
> *And anguished poets doing themselves in*

I didn't hear back from him again. Perhaps while I was bent over my phone Milner had returned without my noticing. It was a small start, but a significant one, I felt. I swallowed down the rest of my lukewarm chocolate and headed off home with a tiny flutter of happiness about my heart.

I thought Gladwell and I would soon be in full flow of communication once more. But it was not to be. What seemed like a long time passed without further contact, and I was returned to my previous state of agonised ignorance. I couldn't concentrate, I couldn't eat, I hardly slept, I was worse than ever. I didn't understand what was the matter with me.

Around this time an old school friend got in touch out of the blue and we arranged to meet up at the local Pizza Express near where I worked. We had not been terribly close all those years before, but we had shared a certain sardonic sense of humour coupled with a jaundiced outlook on the institutionalised environment in which we found ourselves. We had actually collaborated for a short while on the school magazine, until we were thrown off the committee by the goody-two-shoes who far outnumbered us, for what they saw as our subversive and cynical attitude. Hal had then proposed that we write our own alternative rag, a sort of parody, I suppose, of the official one. We had some fun producing it and thought ourselves hugely superior, but it wasn't actually all that good. There was some nasty stuff about various teachers and pupils—most of it instigated by him, I have to say—and after distributing fifty or a hundred copies we were hauled up in front of the headmaster and threatened with expulsion. Of course, he had no intention of imposing any such punishment, but he did force us to publish an embarrassing apology, after which I didn't care to have any more to do with my partner in slime.

Like the narcissist he was, Hal remained under the impression that we were best friends. He still seemed to think so, in fact, after the more than fifteen years in which we had had no contact and I, for one, had barely thought of him. A mutual acquaintance in the Arts Council had put him onto me; I was sure he would never have found me otherwise. The thought of meeting up bored me slightly, but feeling a bit sorry for him, and vaguely flattered by his interest, I conceded one of my evenings to his company.

The years had been kind to him, perhaps overly

kind: with his jeans and t-shirt and his curly hair he still resembled a schoolboy on his way to a rock concert. He jumped up and greeted me with frothing enthusiasm. "Hey, Timmy! How're ya doin'?" The fake accent reminded me keenly of what a generalised prat he used to be.

"Hey," I replied, slapping him on the arm with equally fake friendliness, "only my mother calls me Timmy."

"Purely ironic, man; purely ironic. How're ya doin'? Sit down, sit down. Let me get you a beer." He signalled the waitress. "Can you get my friend here a—what will you have? Get him a San Miguel."

"I'll have an orange juice, please," I told her.

"You're kidding," Hal said when she had gone. "You on medication or something?"

"No. I just don't drink."

"Wow. OK. So—what? You're all into clean living nowadays?"

"Not especially. I just don't like alcohol all that much."

"What, you don't *like* it? Or you don't like the effect it has on you?" Annoyed by his line of questioning, I didn't reply. He hardly noticed. "Always had to be in control, didn't you, Nesbitt? I remember that about you. Never one to let your hair down—oops, sorry!" He ran a caressing hand over his locks.

"Why don't we order something?" I said tightly. We consulted our menus. The waitress returned with my orange juice and we both ordered pizzas. For a while we chatted pleasantly about old times, former schoolmates I had almost forgotten but he, for reasons best known to himself, had kept up with, old teachers, old enemies, long-ago escapades. Hal started on his second beer.

"So, you're a minion of the evil bureaucracy that is the Arts Council? I hope you're working to bring the system down from within."

"Absolutely. And you?"

"Oh, I'm definitely outside the system. I'd never let those bastards get their hands on me." He swigged his beer.

"What do you do for a living?"

"I work for myself. Always have. At least that way the only bastard you have to answer to is you." He broke open a breadstick and proceeded to wolf it down. "You name it, I've sold it. Stairlifts, pool tables, double glazing. Right now I'm into hot tubs."

"And is there a great call for—hot tubs?"

"You'd be amazed. I go all over the country. Everybody wants a hot tub. Bank managers, bricklayers, little old ladies. Footballers' wives." He gave a filthy grin.

"You know, I never saw you as a salesman," I admitted.

"What did you see me as?"

"Oh, I don't know." I thought back to our nasty little school rag. "Maybe a journalist."

"No way! Far too much like hard work. Want to know what I saw you as?"

"Not really."

"Exactly what you are. Except that would only be a front for something secret and mysterious."

"What do you mean?"

"I don't know. Except that you always seemed that way. Kind of bland and innocuous on the outside, but underneath—something much more deep and sinister."

"I don't know why you would think that."

"Go on—tell me. You've got something else going on. Are you working for MI5?"

I laughed uncomfortably. Our pizzas arrived.

"Didn't you have ideas of being a writer?" Hal persisted, carving his up with gusto. A strong smell of hot cheese, warm dough and pepperoni wafted towards me. I felt slightly nauseous.

"Didn't *you*?"

"Not likely. What did I say about hard work? No, but you were serious, as I recall. That stuff you wrote for the magazine was pretty good."

I shrugged. "Lots of people dream of being writers. Life takes over."

"Shame. I always hoped you'd become a bestselling novelist. Then I could say I knew somebody famous." He shoved one large piece of pizza after another between his lips and talked with his mouth full. "Anyway, we're still young, aren't we? There's time. I don't intend to be selling hot tubs when I'm fifty."

"What do you intend to be doing?"

"Sitting in one, hopefully! Preferably on the Costa del Sol." He called for the waitress and ordered another beer. "So where are you living these days?"

"Crouch End," I lied.

"Nice. Very posh. Any—er—live-in services?"

"I beg your pardon?"

"Got the place to yourself?"

"Yes."

"No significant other, then?"

"No."

"Oh." He looked down at his plate, as if completely absorbed by his pizza. I toyed with my margherita, which was largely uneaten. "So—er ... Which side did you land on, in the end?"

"Come again?"

"Girls or boys?" He smiled up at me. "Or both? I could see you going for both."

"Mind your own fucking business," I said, amiably.

"Oh, come on. Don't be such a prude." A sudden idea struck him. "Or is it neither?" Peering into my face, he said, "It's neither, isn't it? Fuck! You poor bastard."

"Fuck off."

"Listen, I don't blame you. People are more trouble than they're worth. All those *relationship* complications. But still. You don't have to let it get complicated, you know. I can put you onto a service, very discreet, very classy, very sensitive, caters to all tastes—and I mean all. Mention my name, they might even give you a discount—"

"You really don't get the message, do you? If you don't drop it right now I may have to leave."

He held up his hands in a gesture of surrender. "Whoa! There's no need to get your knickers in a twist. Pardon me, Miranda. I didn't realise it was such a touchy subject." I half-rose from my seat. "Sit down. I'll shut up about it, I promise. It's none of my business." I sat down again. He got back to sawing at his food. "I guess it's all part of that double-life shtick of yours."

"Any double life I may seem to have is entirely the product of your own imagination."

Hal brayed, and for a little while we consumed our food in silence. I reflected angrily that it had been a complete mistake to meet with him. I should have listened to my gut instinct. The guy was a wanker; always had been, always would be. Time doesn't change people, on the whole, but I was only just beginning to learn that life-lesson. Then he said something stunning and unexpected.

"Hey, talking of writers—did you ever read that guy's blog—the parody guy?"

"Parody guy?" I repeated, in a cold, small voice.

"Yeah—whatsisname. Gladwell. Gladwell the Parodist. Did you ever read that blog?"

"I don't think so."

"Oh, you should. He does what we did, only much better. Fucking brilliant. I highly recommend it."

"I'll seek it out," I said. A huge wave of nausea washed over me. I set down my knife and fork. "Excuse me."

I hurried to the men's, bent over the toilet bowl and retched. Nothing emerged, and I straightened up shortly and stood leaning against the stall, panting. I had broken out in a sweat on my face and neck. I tried to identify what it was I was feeling. Violated: yes, that was it. The idea of him reading Gladwell's blog—*our* blog—the sound of Gladwell's name coming from his lips, made me feel raped and violated.

I went to the sink and splashed my face with cold water. For a few moments I stood gazing at my own reflection in the mirror as the drops trickled down my nose and chin. There were droplets of water in my eyelashes. I hardly recognised myself. I was ugly, I knew it, middle age was creeping up on me, there were flaps of loose flesh along my jaw and I was growing bald. No-one, man or woman, would look twice at me but Hal was right, there was something in the eyes that spoke of more, something secret and interior. But you had to look carefully to see it.

I wiped my face dry hastily with a paper towel and staggered back to the table. Hal had finished his pizza and ordered another beer. He looked up at me with concern. "You OK?"

"Yes, I'm fine. Just getting over a stomach bug."

"You should have said. We could have put this off to another time."

"I'll be fine. I just—I don't mean to be rude, but I really need to get home and go to bed."

"Sure. Don't worry about it. You go home and get some rest." I pulled a couple of notes out of my wallet. "No, mate—I'll get this one. Seriously. You can get the next."

The idea of there being a next sent a fresh wave of sickness pulsing through me, and I insisted and laid the notes down on the table.

"What about your pizza? Shall we get you a doggy bag? No? Then do you mind if I - ?" He forked it. "Listen—take my card. We'll do this again some time when you're feeling better."

"Sure, sure," I said, and took his card. Hal Babcock, Sales, Regal Hot Tubs.

"And if you fancy a hot tub, I can do you a sweet deal," he added.

I left the restaurant and began walking swiftly away towards the tube. I was about halfway there when my phone vibrated. It was a message from Gladwell.

> *Antinous. Meet me? 9pm Tuesday, World's End, Camden.*
> *G.*

I reached home in a state of hysteria.

— XV —

Three days after my interview with Rob Collins, I was walking home from the tube when I spotted a police car parked around the corner from my flat. It was something or nothing—very likely nothing—but taking sudden fright I turned on my heel and started back the way I had come with my heart pounding.

I didn't stop until I reached the High Street. There I stepped into the first café and, heavily out of breath and not knowing entirely what I was doing, ordered a glass of milk. For the next hour I sat and watched the door, half-expecting a pair of plain clothes officers to walk in and arrest me, but nothing happened, of course. My hands shook; my mind was a torrent of fear and apprehension. Suddenly the risks I had been running seemed terribly real. I harangued myself mentally for being a fool, I cursed Collins for a suspicious swine. It was my interview with him that had been the tipping point. Perhaps they were all in collusion: all the friends of Ralph I had been to see, working in concert to corner and accuse me. Maybe instead of playing them, as I had complacently thought, I was the one who had been played all along.

But that made no sense. They couldn't possibly be that sophisticated. Besides, I reminded myself, it was I who had pursued them, not the other way around. I had placed myself in this predicament. And yet I felt hunted down, hounded, persecuted. It was as if, at some profound level, I was not to blame.

When the hour was up I decided to go back and check whether the coast was clear. I took my street as casually as I could. The police car was gone, and no-one was waiting suspiciously in any of the parked vehicles. I entered the building, inserting my key in the lock with trembling fingers. Once upstairs I slammed the door to and released a deep, shaky sigh. The flat was quiet and still, just as I had left it.

It must have been ten minutes before I came to and realised I had been standing paralysed, my mind a blank. I stripped, took a quick shower and put on a fresh outfit. I ate some tomato soup; it was all I could stomach. Then I pulled down my holdall from the top of the wardrobe and stuffed in as many of my clothes as I could manage.

In truth, I had very little idea what I was doing. I didn't know where I was going or for how long. Vague notions of Goa and Bali floated through my mind. Living was cheap there, or so I had heard, and my few savings might keep me going a while. But the whole situation felt unreal. Part of me, knowing I was innocent, didn't believe in the need for any of this.

When I did finally leave the flat, lock the door behind me and walk downstairs, I moved like an automaton. I made my way briskly to the tube as if I were setting off for work. I had taken this journey so many hundreds of times that until reaching Victoria I remained in a dream. I didn't come to, in fact, until I found myself standing in front of the departures board in the mainline station, wondering to myself which train to catch. There was a train to Bognor leaving in eight minutes.

So much for Bali.

So much for adulthood and independence, I thought to myself as the train moved out of the station. So much for coolness and professionalism and self-possession. You kidded yourself that you could handle all this on your own. But when the crisis comes you still run home to Mummy.

Seated in the corner of the carriage, watching the semi-rural scene flash by, I became mesmerised by my own reflection hanging in the glass. It looked haunted and unfamiliar. How far had I come, what strange changes had I gone through, what was happening to me? I felt my whole life being sucked away into a whirling nothingness. The remarkable thing was that for a brief spell, while on that journey, I was glad of it. I felt liberated, and as the train flashed on through the Sussex countryside there was nothing I wanted more than to leave my whole life behind and be given up to whatever chaos and desolation awaited me.

The euphoria dissipated somewhat when the train stopped and let me out onto the station at Bognor Regis. It was a soft September day, sunny and windless; I decided to walk the half-mile to my parents' house. Long before I got there I was drenched in sweat. With my heavy holdall banging at my knee I marched up the garden path and rang the bell. I hadn't stopped to think what effect my sudden, unannounced arrival would have on my over-anxious mother.

I must have looked pretty bad, because when she opened the front door her mouth fell open. "Hello, Mum." She stood there staring at me. I attempted a smile. "Aren't you going to let me in?"

"What is it? What's happened?"

"Nothing. Nothing's happened. Can't I come in?"

"I'm in the middle of cleaning."

"So?"

"But you look a sight!"

I felt annoyed. It was not the welcome I had looked for or needed. "Well, I won't mess up your carpet. I'll take my shoes off." She stood aside then, and I did so and came in.

My father was out the back, painting his boat. I guessed this was his usual place of banishment while my mother turned the house upside down with mops and buckets and dusters and vacuum cleaners. How the precious hours of life get wasted, I thought as I dropped my holdall and edged my way through to the kitchen. "I'm really thirsty," I said, fetching a glass and filling it at the tap. As I gulped it down my mother repeated, "You look terrible."

"I'm fine. Why don't you get back to your cleaning? I'll take a bit of a lie down, if that's OK."

Leaving my used glass on the kitchen counter I pushed past her and made my way upstairs to the guest room. There were no sheets on the bed. I lay down on the bare mattress and listened to my parents moving around and talking downstairs. Eventually the vacuum cleaner started up and I realised gratefully that they were going to leave me in peace, at least for the time being. I closed my eyes.

The moment I did so, however, I was suddenly overcome by fears of all kinds. I could hardly name or identify them, they swarmed with such speed and complexity through my brain. It was like being overrun by mental ants. My skin crawled; my whole body twitched. I sat up quickly, yanking my eyes open by sheer force of will. Assuming an upright foetal position, I began chewing primitively on my own hand.

What the hell was happening to me? My heart raced, my mouth was dry, my palms sweated. I was terrified.

In an effort to calm myself I jumped up off the bed and began pacing around the small half-furnished bedroom. As I did so I noticed the artificial, unused smell, the same that had filled Ralph Gladwell's childhood room, which was also small and sparsely furnished like this: the room of someone who rarely returned *and now*, my mind insisted on adding, *never would*, a room that waited hopefully and mournfully. And it was as though I were feeling the reality of his death all over again for the first time, emerging from a state of numbed shock to an unfamiliar one of grief, guilt and fear.

I drew several deep breaths and attempted to rationalise. In all these past weeks I had been driven by one ambition, to lay hands on the manuscripts of Gladwell's youthful novels. I had, in fact, hazarded my own fate for the sake of them. I knew beyond reasonable doubt that they existed; indeed, Aaron Milner had confirmed as much. But what if I were destined never to track them down? And worse yet - what if my pursuit of them were to be the cause of my own downfall? In that case, Gladwell would have won. From beyond the grave, Gladwell would have beaten me.

I dined with my parents that evening in near silence. There was so little I could tell them, so little they could ask. My mother I caught glancing at me every so often with a frightened look, and in my new mood of revelation I wondered, Is she really afraid of me? During that other strange time, the time of my previous obsession, I'd never given her feelings towards me a moment's thought. Now I began as it were to see myself from the outside, and a shudder went through me. But it was too painful and confusing; I pushed it away.

As for my father, he sat bent over his plate in his usual attitude of taciturn self-absorption, not pleased to see me, I reckoned, but not likely, either, to let it put a crimp on his important activities. The weather was good, and for the next couple of days he was outside painting his boat almost from morning till night. My mother waited on him like a servant. I lay upstairs in the stuffy little bedroom thinking and thinking until I felt myself disappearing into a vortex as tiny and tight as a pinhole. I switched my phone on and switched it off again; I paced the room like a prisoner awaiting execution.

On the morning of the third day there came a tentative knock at the door. I said, "Come in," though I hardly knew how I got my vocal chords to work. Enter my mother, still staring at me as if she had seen a ghost. Irritated, I turned away and kept up my pacing. "Timmy, Timmy," she said, "won't you tell me what's the matter?"

I stopped by the window and looked down into the suburban street with its neat houses, its tidy flower beds. How I wished its mundanity could soothe my fear, or calm the brittle beating of my heart. "You wouldn't understand. It's nothing you can help me with."

"Have you done something, are you in trouble?"

I emitted a hard, short laugh. "Done something! Yes, I think you could say I've done something."

"Oh, Timmy—what have you done?"

Her tone was so heartbroken it brought me to a sense of compunction. I approached and hugged her. "Don't worry, Mum. It will all be over soon."

"What will? What do you mean?"

"I'll sort it all out. But I might have to go away for a little while."

"Where to?"

"I can't tell you that. It depends," I smiled involuntarily, "on whether they arrest me."

"Oh, God, Timmy!"

"Now, don't get all hysterical. They haven't a shred of evidence. I've just acted rather foolishly and brought suspicion on myself."

"Suspicion of what? What do they think you've done?"

The idea of answering this out loud got me pacing again and rubbing my palms together. "Well—murder, I'm afraid!" I laughed nervously.

"Oh, God!" My mother collapsed onto the bed. She began to weep.

I stood watching her, not knowing what more to say. And then my father entered. He looked tousled and exhausted. There were smears of paint on his overalls. Clearly, painting his boat for the sixteenth time was taking its toll. "What's going on here?"

"Nothing!" I replied carelessly.

"Why is your mother crying, then?" He stared down at her. "What's the matter, Brenda?"

"They think—our Timmy—m-murdered—somebody!"

My father threw me an angry and accusing look. I was reminded of occasions when I had come home from school with a note for my parents to visit the headmaster. Had I, or had I not, played hooky the previous Wednesday?

"And have you?" my father asked.

I burst out laughing. "Well, thank you, Father, for that vote of confidence!"

"Don't you come all clever-clever with me. Look at the state your mother's in. This is no laughing matter."

"Hardly, since I'm the one in trouble."

He sat down on the bed, put his arms around my mother and attempted to comfort her. "Come on, now, Brenda. Pull yourself together." This only induced a renewed bout of wailing.

"Nice work, Dad. That's really going to help."

My father was puce with rage. "How dare you put her through all this again! You spoiled, selfish, self-indulgent little brat!"

Red eyed, my mother protested, "Oh, please, Gordon—please. Don't make everything worse!"

He rose suddenly. "I'm calling the police."

Both I and my mother started at these words.

"If the police want to interview him they should interview him. Proper process should be followed."

"I never said they wanted to interview me." If he'd made for the phone right then I would have been ready to kill him.

"What are you doing here, then?"

"Looking for a little parental sympathy, though I should have known better."

"Sympathy for murdering someone, I have to tell you, you're unlikely to receive."

"So now I'm a murderer, tried and convicted by my own father. Thank you very much!"

"How am I to know? You're capable of it."

"I will be in a minute."

"*Please!*" my mother begged, tearing her hair. "I can't bear it! I can't!"

She was hysterical. Sobered, we pulled up short. A few moments' silence were broken only by her sobs.

"Anyway," I said eventually, "it was clearly a mistake to come here. At least I can put that right." I picked up my holdall and made for the door.

"No, don't go! Timmy, don't go. I'm frightened!"

Kneeling down, I held her hands. "Don't be frightened, Mum. I'll be OK. Honest."

"But where are you going?"

"Somewhere safe."

"Don't disappear. Timmy, please don't disappear."

"All right, Mum." I kissed her. "I promise I won't disappear."

She clung to me desperately. It was only with some effort that I could pull myself away. I left the room without so much as a glance at my father.

I was on my way out of the front door when he appeared downstairs. He didn't attempt to prevent my departure; he only said, "Tell me: are the police after you?"

"Of course not."

"Then why all this?"

I shrugged my shoulders.

"Why don't you just go to them and explain, if it's all a misunderstanding?"

"It's complicated."

"All right, then. At least take some money, if you're going to go walkabout." He reached into his pocket. I stayed him.

"I have money." I made for the door, hesitated and added, "Just take care of Mum."

Then I left the house.

I returned to the station, walking fast, my mind a maelstrom of disconnected thoughts. Visiting my parents had been a mistake all right, yet somehow it had felt necessary. I tried to identify the impulse that had taken me there. This was the end game, I told myself. The story would soon be over; the hounds were closing in. I had gone to see them in order to say good bye.

It was not until I reached the station that I began to ask myself where I was headed next. I paused by the departures board and stared at it for a good five minutes, weighing up the various destinations. London held no interest. Brighton likewise. At last I approached the window and paid in cash for a single to Portsmouth. I would catch the next available ferry and take things from there.

There was a wait of twenty-five minutes for the train, so I sat down on a bench and prepared to while away the time with a tabloid newspaper that was lying there. But everything my eye fell upon was so ugly and stupid and distasteful that I soon flung it down in disgust. I was filled with revulsion for the world; not the world of nature that I saw burgeoning in the late summer sunshine, the last butterflies and hyrandines that would soon be dying or leaving for warmer climes, but the grimy, secret, hypocritical world of human beings who envied and despised and trampled on all that was beautiful and sweet, and to which I too belonged.

I had not intended to switch on my phone—for all I knew, I was being traced by means of it—but out of sheer idleness and in a mood of perversity I did so now and checked for messages. There were only two: one from work, no doubt wondering where I was, and one from Ralph Gladwell's mother. It read as follows:

> *Dear Mr Tate*
> *While sorting through the attic I have come across some manuscripts of Ralph's that may be of interest. If you would like to examine them, do get back to me and we will arrange a time.*
> *Best regards,*
> *Eileen Gladwell*

It was surely a sign. I hurried back to the window and bought a ticket to London.

— XVI —

I ARRIVED AT THE World's End shortly before nine p.m. and made a quick scan of the bar; there was no sign of Gladwell. I got myself a tonic water and found a seat with a good view of the entrance.

I was extremely nervous. This meeting went against my every instinct. In fact, I had almost not come at all. Sitting at my kitchen table, I had waited until the very last moment to set off. Finally, I grabbed my jacket and half-ran out of the flat on a sort of suicidal impulse. There was a deep misgiving in my heart which told me this could not possibly end well and might even lead to some dreadful catastrophe.

Nor did I truly believe Gladwell would show. He was notorious for missing appointments, and if he had dropped his message to me in the wake of some tiff with Milner, as I was sure he had, there was every chance he had forgotten all about it within the hour. The urge to see Antinous would have died along with the spite or jealousy that had inspired it. By now the two of them would be lovey-dovey again.

But I was wrong: at five past nine Gladwell arrived, looking smart in a black suit and with freshly-washed hair flowing down over his shoulders. A number of heads turned as he entered; wherever he went he had that star quality. But he seemed a little unsure of himself tonight, glancing around the bar and hesitating. He was looking for me, of course, and didn't know what I looked like. I realised, with sudden poignancy, that this was my last opportunity to remain anonymous. My cover blown, I would lose whatever mystique I possessed in Gladwell's mind, and the title Antinous would become a joke.

I rose, crossed the bar, and introduced myself.

There was slight surprise in his look, but not the revulsion I had anticipated. Indeed, his expression quickly altered to a sort of relief. It was as though he had finally encountered someone he had long been looking for and even expecting. I thought I saw there, too, a hint of sadness, along with that almost unquantifiable loss of authority I had detected earlier, and of which perhaps only someone like me, who had observed him now so obsessively and for so long, would have been aware. I felt a pang which I can only describe as joy.

"What can I get you to drink?" I asked.

"Oh, I don't know," he replied vaguely, peering towards the bar. "I don't know what they have. I've never been here before." I ordered him a pint, and we retired to my table.

"I don't ever come to Camden," Gladwell said, still peering about as if afraid of spotting someone he knew. "That's why I wanted to meet here. I don't want to run into anybody."

"No; it's not one of my hang-outs, either."

"We should be all right, then." He seemed to relax a little, and took a sip of beer. "It's good of you to come."

"My pleasure."

"I didn't think you'd agree to it. You're so mysterious."

"One can't go on being mysterious for ever."

"I suppose not." His leg was jiggling in an unconscious expression of anxiety; he was a far cry from his usual ebullient self. As for me, I was paralysed by shyness, as I'd always known I would be.

"How are things?" I asked eventually.

"Well..." He turned his glass. "I think Aaron and I are going to split up."

"I'm sorry to hear it."

"Are you?" He threw me a piercing glance. "Everybody I know seems to think he's wrong for me."

"But that's none of their business, is it? I mean, if you care for him…"

"I love him. But that doesn't mean he's right for me."

I took refuge in my tonic water.

"He's shallow, selfish, ignorant, immature," Gladwell went on, "and totally gorgeous. I love him with all my heart and soul. I'll never get over it."

"But he doesn't love you?" I hazarded.

He choked, and couldn't answer.

"I'm sorry. That was tactless."

"No; I need to face it. He doesn't love me. He couldn't love me and do the things he does." He sighed deeply. "I need to get out of there, for the sake of my self-respect."

"Where will you go?"

"Back to my own place. I just lost my tenant. Which seems timely."

We sat in silence for a few moments.

"So!" Gladwell suddenly interjected, in the tone of one determinedly changing the subject. "We meet at last." And he smiled, wolflike, showing his white teeth.

"We meet at last," I echoed.

"My mystery man. Antinous." Still smiling, he looked me up and down.

"It's Jim."

"You know, you're quite a talented chap. Don't be embarrassed. I mean it. I've really enjoyed your efforts."

"Thank you."

"You sound offended."

"Not at all."

"I know I haven't been on the ball lately. I've neglected the blog. Hell, I haven't even been tweeting. The fact is" (he began methodically destroying a beer mat) "I've been too tired. All this with Aaron, all the scenes, it's tremendously draining. I can't begin to tell you. I used to thrive on that sort of thing, but I must be getting too old for it. I'm exhausted, Antinous. Do you know what I mean?" He ripped the mat in half. "How can you, you're still young. You can't imagine."

I deferred to his greater knowledge of exhaustion.

"I'd like to go away for a long holiday. Would you like to come away with me? Of course not, you have your own life to lead. I wish I could rid myself of—me! I get so tired of myself sometimes." He looked up suddenly, perhaps noticing my silence. "But I didn't mean to burden you with my troubles. Tell me something. Tell me about yourself."

"There's not much to say. I'm a very boring person."

"I don't believe that. Nobody with a talent like yours can be completely boring. Tell me, did you ever aspire to writing anything proper?"

"How do you mean?"

"You know—proper writing. Fiction, essays, poetry. The truly creative stuff." He snorted, and added, "As opposed to the destructive."

"I didn't think you regarded parody as destructive."

"Don't I?"

"I thought you saw it as a service to literature."

"Do I, indeed!"

"That's what you said."

"What I said—when?" His eyes narrowed.

I recovered myself. "Many times. On the blog. On the internet."

"Doubtless. I'm always repeating myself." He downed his beer. "Let me tell you something about me. When I was a teenager—a young man—the only thing I desired in the whole world, other than lots of sex, was to become a great novelist. I was convinced it was my destiny. Written in the stars! All I had to do was write and write and strive and I would get there. The world would acknowledge me. And do you know what happened?"

I looked at him questioningly.

"Well, it may have escaped your notice. Nothing happened! The world laughed in my face. Which is to say, certain readers for certain literary agents and publishers' editors laughed in my face. Metaphorically speaking. And why do you think that was?"

"Because you didn't have the right contacts?"

"No, sweet Antinous. No, sweet, loyal Antinous. It was because I was *no bloody good*!" He laughed, a loud Gladwellian laugh, one that made several heads turn. "That's the simple truth. For years I blamed it on everyone else, on their stupidity and blindness, on their crass lack of appreciation, on the evil times we live in culturally, but at the end of the day, when you write and write and write and get turned down and turned down and turned down there is only one logical conclusion you can come to, and that is that you are just no good. Would you like another drink?"

"Uh—thanks. A tonic water. With ice."

He picked up our empty glasses and dragged himself heavily to the bar. I remained seated, trying to come to terms with the conversation I was having. There was still something unreal about the whole situation. I couldn't quite believe I was speaking with Gladwell face to face and that he was confiding all these deeply personal matters.

"So!" he continued, thunking his tall frame down again and sliding my glass toward me. "Now you know the dark and bitter truth, that Gladwell the Parodist is a failure, a failed writer, the creator of the very stuff he parodies. Not simply a parodist, in fact, but a walking cliché."

"I don't agree with that."

"That's kind of you, sweetie, but nevertheless. I became a parodist out of anger, fury, out of sheer frustration. Out of jealousy and despair that I couldn't create the things I was parodying."

"But you could," I pointed out, "and you did."

He was on a roll; he ignored me. "All parody is written out of two motives: admiration and envy. Without admiration one can't feel envy, and without envy one doesn't know how to despise. But the best parody is written out of deep, inner pain, the pain of the failed writer. Which is how I know you have tried to write, even if you won't admit to it."

"I'll take that as a compliment."

"You should. But I feel sorry for you, just as I feel sorry for myself." He sat silently for a while, staring into his beer, and I waited for him to continue. I have always preferred listening to speaking. "I'll let you into a secret, Antinous: I love literature. I worship it. It gives my life meaning. But I also hate it, because I can't produce it. What did Hopkins say? *But strain, Time's eunuch, and not breed one work that wakes.*" Gladwell had written a hilarious parody of Hopkins a few years back; I had laughed myself into hiccoughs over it. "Of course," he added, "what Hopkins really needed was to shag a few beautiful young seminarians, but that aside, I know where he was coming from."

"What did you do with your writings?"

"My writings?"

"Your novels and so on. Did you destroy them?"

"No, dear heart: I treasure them. They are my children. Even though I should have drowned them at birth!" He chuckled; then his face dropped. "That's one of the reasons I hoped Aaron and I would stay together till the end. He was going to burn them for me, after I was gone."

"The manuscripts?"

"Yes; and the disks. To defy posterity." He had a sudden thought. "You should read them, Antinous. They'd give you a good laugh!"

"I'd like that very much."

"Only on one condition, though: that I get to read yours."

"Oh, I haven't anything much for you to read."

"No, no." He took a long drink of beer and slammed down his glass. "You get to laugh at me, I get to laugh at you. That's only fair."

I sat silent, my mind racing. No way in a million years was I ever going to show him my half-finished opus. "I might not laugh," I said finally.

Gladwell ignored me; he was glancing about the bar again, not in an anxious but in a predatory way. I saw, by the manner in which he cast his eyes up and down the figures of one or two young men, that his mind was no longer on matters literary. A flicker of extreme annoyance ran through me, not only because of what he had just said but because I felt snubbed. If he was going to be with me, I said to myself, then let him be with me. I wasn't going to sit there watching while he sized up the local talent. But I was reluctant to admit that I was feeling jealous.

"Well," I said, exaggeratedly consulting my watch, "I should probably be getting back."

"Oh! Must you?"

"Well, I..."

"I'd thought we would stay much longer, or... Must you go, Antinous?"

He was hard to resist. Something about those eyes, turned on you with all their affection and interest and desire, made you feel as though, for that moment, you were the most special person in the world. To be wanted by someone so charismatic made you almost drunk with joy.

"I must," I repeated, drawing on all my strength.

"Alas." He smiled sadly. "But we'll meet again?"

"If you really want to."

"If I really want to! Sweetie, there's nothing I want more."

I smiled too. "Then we will." He seized my hand; I was afraid he was going to kiss it, so I snatched it back. Then I rose and departed with a feigned nonchalance which must have left him reeling.

All the way home my mind was a scrambled confusion of thoughts and impressions which I couldn't begin to make sense of or piece together. What on earth was Gladwell up to? Was he really trying to seduce me, or was that just his way with everyone? Could he really not see how unattractive I was? It was baffling. The only explanation must be that he was hoping to make Milner jealous; either that or he was on the rebound. I reached my flat in East Finchley without being fully conscious of how I had got there. My heart was beating fast and I felt as though I had been walking on air.

— XVII —

SIX WEEKS AFTER MY original visit to Ralph Gladwell's childhood home in High Wycombe, I found myself back in that neat suburban street with its regimented gardens and net curtains, its clipped lawns, clean driveways and immaculate front doors. It was early September and the first chill of autumn was in the air, but the sun shone and the light had a watery clearness. I stood for several minutes outside the house with the magnolia tree and the twin gables, breathing in the scent of a few late roses and relishing the feeling of suppressed excitement now churning in my chest. Drawing a deep breath I walked up to the porch and rang the bell.

Mrs Gladwell opened the door. She was as smart and well-dressed as ever, in a sky-blue blouse and black slacks which flattered her figure, and her hair was crisp and brilliant as though she had just come from the hairdresser. She gave a small start on seeing me.

"Oh, Mr Tate! I wasn't expecting you so soon."

"I'm sorry. I should have called first. I hope it isn't inconvenient."

"No… Of course not." She gave a little smile, but made no move to admit me.

"Er—might I come in?"

"Yes, of course. Sorry."

"Call me Jim," I reminded her brightly as I stepped

over the threshold. I thought she might be nervous about showing me the manuscripts, about possibly parting with them. I wanted to put her at her ease and reassure her.

"Jim. Yes. Sorry. Jim." She hovered in the hallway, oddly discomfited, as if she'd forgotten the layout of her own home.

"Shall we - ?" I suggested, indicating the lounge.

"Yes—of course." We went through. I looked around greedily, expecting to see a pile of manuscripts on the coffee table. But there was nothing there.

"Can I get you some tea?" she said.

"No, thank you."

To my annoyance, she then invited me to sit down. I was tired of all this shilly-shallying. I wanted those manuscripts.

"And how have you been keeping, Mr—Jim?"

"Very well, thank you. And you?"

"Oh, well—you know. Managing as best I can."

"I'm sure it hasn't been easy."

"No. It hasn't been easy." She perched on the very edge of the armchair, her knees pressed together and her hands clasped so tightly the knuckles had turned white. She glanced toward the window and my eyes followed. There was nothing there but the top of an azalea bush peeking over the sill.

I cleared my throat and said, "So. I gather you've been doing some clearing out?"

"Yes. With—what's happened, I felt that it was time to—you know."

"Yes."

"To put the house in order. In case... So everything should be in order. And to give me something else to focus on."

"Of course." I tried my best to be patient. She was his mother, after all.

"It was a lot harder than I expected. All those memories. Painful. Terribly, terribly painful." She looked at me suddenly with red, flaming, accusatory eyes.

"I can imagine."

"I wonder. All Ralph's childhood—up there, in the attic. His things. Toys. Christmas decorations he made. School projects. Did you ever consider he was a little child once?"

"I... I don't..."

"That he had a mother who loved him more than anything in the world?" Her voice was choked and her eyes blazed. It was possible she was accusing me—yes, even probable. But if there was the least chance she had what I was looking for, I didn't care.

"I'm so very sorry for your loss," I said.

She rose abruptly, and seemed to take hold of herself by sheer force of will. "You want to see the *manuscripts*," she added in a new tone, an almost haughty and disdainful one.

"I do. Very much."

"They're upstairs."

"Very well, then." I smiled. "Shall we go upstairs?"

Again she seemed not to know where upstairs was. She stood; I stood; we lingered, facing each other. I indicated the door.

"After you."

She moved to the door like a robot, and I followed her out into the hall and up the stairs. All the bedroom doors were closed. Somewhat to my surprise, on our reaching the landing, Mrs Gladwell fetched a step ladder from the spare bedroom and placed it under the hatch to the loft. Standing aside, she gestured towards it with an expressionless face.

"Up there?" I said. I am not fond of ladders.

She neither moved nor spoke, nor did the wooden mask of her face alter.

"You didn't bring them downstairs?" I asked, a touch querulously, and she shook her head. All my instincts told me that something here was not right. But I was unwilling to listen to my instincts. I was too hard driven by my desires, by the thought that the manuscripts I had been seeking so obsessively might now lie a few feet above my head.

I placed my foot on the first rung of the ladder, drew a deep breath and began to climb.

It was a light aluminium ladder which wobbled slightly under my weight, but she made no effort to hold it steady for me. She remained planted where she was, staring fixedly at me with those big hawk's eyes, Ralph's eyes, red and accusing, and I went on climbing until I pushed open the hatch and my head emerged into the warm stuffy air of the loft space.

I saw immediately that the loft, lit by single bare bulb which hung from the rafters, was packed to the gills with all sorts of junk, old clothes, old curtains, old electrical goods, stacks of cardboard boxes filled with God knows what; the very sight of it overwhelmed me. I felt a sort of dragging at my heart, but I couldn't turn back now, and heavily, clumsily, like a landed flounder, I dragged myself up from the top of the ladder into the attic, acquiring a long dusty streak down my jacket and trousers for my pains. The ladder rocked so dangerously it almost fell. Mrs Gladwell did then step forward instinctively to right it, but remained at its foot, gazing silently up at me with baleful eyes. She made no move to follow as I'd expected.

"Are you not coming?" I called down through the hole. I dusted myself off as best I could, straightened up and promptly banged my head. The sloping roof was so low even somebody of my height could only stoop. "There's an awful lot of stuff up here. Could you give me some pointers?" But there was no answer, and when I looked down again, Mrs Gladwell had vanished. It was then that I heard the murmur of her voice downstairs. She must have been speaking on the telephone.

Something told me I should get the hell out of there, and right away. But surveying the sea of Gladwell's possessions I was unable to restrain myself. The manuscripts! They could really be here.

I just needed a little time, I told myself. Just a little time. I determined to be as methodical as possible. The likelihood was that the manuscripts lay close to the entrance. I would start there and work outwards in concentric circles.

It was frightening, I thought as I began hunting through boxes of books and clothes and miscellaneous parts to gadgets no longer functioning, just how much junk could accumulate over the course of a life. Defunct toys, unwanted Christmas annuals, a badminton set, a moth-eaten teddy bear; old board games, snakes and ladders, Monopoly, Cluedo; stacked towers of jigsaws I somehow couldn't associate with someone of Ralph's restless intellect. He had never struck me as a person who needed to kill time. "All Ralph's childhood," Mrs Gladwell had said. And yet, knowing how extraordinary a man he was, the very ordinariness of the objects lent them a certain poignancy.

The manuscripts didn't appear to lie within the first circuit of the hatch, so I started on the next. I was thoroughly absorbed now; I had forgotten Mrs Gladwell and her telephone call. I had almost forgotten myself. I was intent on one thing only: my quarry and my prey. Inside one cardboard box I discovered cricket pads, a blazer with a crest and a folder of sixth form English essays, written in a clear, round, schoolboy's hand. I scanned them, embarrassed, with my heart thumping. One was a heartfelt paean to Gerard Manley Hopkins.

I scoured the box to the dregs, but there was nothing more personal in there, neither a postcard nor a poem. In a fit of sentimentality I took the Hopkins essay, folded it and stuffed it into my pocket. I set the box aside and started on the next.

By now I had entirely lost track of time. The attic was warm and muggy; my mouth and lungs were full of dust. I wished I had a glass of water, but was reluctant to give up my search even for a moment. Yet, beyond this, there was something curiously cathartic in this ritual excavation of Ralph's early life, the dead body of his early life, I might have said, if that had not been too morbid. And I seemed to sense the presence of Ralph himself, smiling at something, looking over my shoulder.

There was a taste in my mouth, bloody, metallic, which I recognised as that of extreme hunger; I hadn't eaten all day but it was not hunger for food I was feeling. It was a need even more visceral, a desire which had come nowhere near being sated, which had only been sharpened by the difficulties of my quest. I thought I would be willing to die, then, if I could only fulfil it. I had been ready, after all, to fling myself into any kind of danger.

And then I found the manuscripts.

They lay in the farthest corner, where the eaves were lowest. They were stacked in a neat pile, carefully covered by a plastic bag. There were three typewritten ones, each a couple of inches thick and held together by half-perished rubber bands; the top sheets were dated to a period in Ralph's early to mid-thirties. Below these lay perhaps a dozen foolscap-sized hardback notebooks. On leafing through one or two I found them to be filled with the same round, immature handwriting as that of the school essays: Ralph's juvenilia.

I clutched them to my chest, my arms shaking.

It was high time I made a run for it. Stepping gingerly over the heaps of junk, hugging my prize, I negotiated my way back to the mouth of the attic and looked down. There was no Mrs Gladwell. And there was no ladder.

"Mrs Gladwell!" I called.

I peered down at the green carpet which lay a precipitous ten feet or so below. It was much too far to jump, especially with an armful of manuscripts. If I craned my neck I could see, a little distance away, the step ladder which had been carefully and deliberately moved aside.

"Mrs Gladwell!" I yelled again.

The panic of entrapment overcame me. I am fond of neither heights nor confined spaces. For a third time I screamed, more loudly and hoarsely than ever, this time with real fear in my voice:

"*Mrs Gladwell!!*"

Now someone stepped into view below the hatch, emerging from just beyond my range of vision as if they had been waiting patiently there for me to reach just the right pitch of agitation and alarm. A male someone.

"Now then, Mr Nesbitt. There's no need to shout so loud. We can all hear you. I am Detective Inspector Liddington. Mrs Gladwell is downstairs along with the other officers."

Of course. Of course. I should have expected this. The old cow had betrayed me. Gripping the manuscripts tightly I scanned the attic. No other hatch, no skylight, not even the tiniest chink between the rafters.

"I think you'll find there's only one way down," the policeman continued, clearly relishing the situation, "and that's the same way you went up. Are you still there, Mr Nesbitt? Ah, there you are. Now, just remain calm. If I bring the ladder forward, I would like you to climb down as slowly and quietly as possible. There are two other officers here with me to assist you."

"What do you want with me?" I knew perfectly well, of course. But it was worth playing the innocent.

"Why don't you come on down and we can discuss it." So saying, he lifted the lightweight ladder and planted it squarely under the opening. He was a big, broad-shouldered man in his late thirties. From my vantage point I could see the incipient bald patch on top of his big stupid head.

So the game was up, it seemed. But my manuscripts! What was to become of my manuscripts? I had barely had time to glance at them, and was I to have them snatched away from me so cruelly in my moment of triumph? No—I would rather remain up here. I would rather live here for the rest of my life than come down and be forced to part with them.

"We'd like everything to be done quietly and calmly," Inspector Liddington continued, "but we can come up and bring you down if necessary. I'm sure you wouldn't like us to have to do that." He added, in a patronising tone, "Think of Mrs Gladwell. She's been kind to you, hasn't she? We don't want to upset her, do we?"

"What about my manuscripts?" I demanded, and I hugged them to me as though they were my children.

Something flickered over his upturned face (it was round, puddingy, reddened with the effort of looking up) and he answered, in an even more unctuous tone, "Well, we can talk about those, too, when you come down. We'd just like to talk to you, Timothy—can I call you Timothy? Or is it Tim?"

"Neither, to you," I muttered; he said, "What's that?" and I didn't answer. He was a policeman. He'd come to arrest me. What was there to like? "You can call me John, if you want," he then said, as though I were a suicide on a rooftop. What did he think I was, some kind of nutter?

"All right, I'm coming down," I said, just so he should realise I was perfectly sane.

"That's good, Timothy. That's very good." And he stood back and held the ladder steady. "I'm holding the ladder for you. You can come down now. Slowly and carefully. That's right." I saw two other male figures move into flanking positions, and I turned, placed the manuscripts on the edge of the hatch, and stepped down onto the top of the ladder. Then I picked the manuscripts up again. It wasn't at all easy, climbing down with my booty.

"That's right, that's it," cooed the Inspector, and the moment I planted both feet on the floor, said, "Now, you just give me those."

I pressed the manuscripts more fiercely than ever against my chest, but it was of no use. Three burly figures closed in on me; before I knew it they had the manuscripts, though I cried out wildly, "You aren't taking those!" I hardly knew how it happened, but the next moment they were holding me by the arms and Inspector Liddington was intoning, "Timothy James Nesbitt, I am charging you with the murder of

Ralph Arthur Gladwell on the thirtieth of June. Anything you say may be taken down and used in evidence against you." And they led me away.

— XVIII —

AFTER THAT, GLADWELL AND I met several times at the World's End in Camden. It wasn't a regular thing, and there was no fixed arrangement between us. He contacted me whenever there was some sort of crisis, and since I had very little social life I was generally available. Each time we met he was fulsome in his expressions of gratitude, and each time we parted I had the sense that we might never meet again.

It was over this period that he confided much of what I came to know about his childhood and earlier life. Although not entirely the unvarnished truth (he was incapable of that) the picture he drew was, I believe, more genuine than any he had previously shared. I know this because, especially in telling me about his father, he often repeated that he had never mentioned these matters even to his closest friends. Usually, however, he simply poured out his troubles, so that over time I became privy to the entire unravelling of his relationship with Aaron Milner.

The story was a humdrum and predictable one, but it was a bit heartrending to witness how desperately he tried to believe they would eventually work things out. He see-sawed between unfounded hopes and miserable despair. Milner was a narcissist and a playboy, anybody could see that, and Gladwell himself was under no illusions. But like millions before him, he imagined true love—his trueness of love—would win the day, that he had somehow connected with depths in Milner that didn't actually exist. And then, of course, I was only getting one side of the story. No doubt Gladwell himself was not the entirely innocent party he liked to make out. I listened sympathetically, as was my way, and offered little in the form of comment or advice. Gladwell asked for it, but he didn't really want it.

More than anything, I was agog to read the early novels he had mentioned. However, he didn't seem inclined to bring them up again. Having dangled the carrot in front of me, he seemed to take a perverse pleasure in keeping it out of reach. I tried—rather clumsily, I admit—to bring the conversation round to the subject once or twice, to glean at least something about the novels' subject matter, but to my profound annoyance, they remained linked inexorably, in his mind, to my own unpublished efforts. "Aha!" he would smile, wagging a warning finger. "You laugh at me, I laugh at you, remember! That's the only way!"

I thought, given the enormous amount of tedious heartsearching I'd listened to, that I'd earned my look at the manuscripts five times over, but Gladwell the egotist no doubt regarded my position as a uniquely privileged one. There was no-one, he often declared, with whom he could unburden himself so fully, no-one who would listen with such sympathy and so unjudgmentally, and why? Precisely because I wasn't, in fact, his friend. Friends like Rob Collins repeatedly ripped his throat out, friends like Ray Marriner loved to tear him down; lovers like Anwar Mussa only wanted to start sleeping with him again. It was because I stood outside the charmed circle that he could trust me to be discreet, and most important of all, to have no ulterior motives.

In this way, almost without my realising, I was gradually sucked in. I became as addicted to my meetings with Gladwell as I had once been to receiving his texts and emails, or before that, to reading his blog. Gladwell was my drug of choice. I had been here before. I recognised all the warning signs and I ignored them.

Of course, we didn't only talk about his personal life. We also spoke of his job (which he hated), his friends (about whom he was cynical and amusing) and, naturally, literature and parody. But on this he had curiously little left to say. We would get started on some topic and he would break off, sigh deeply and announce, "Over to you, Antinous." We tried listing the authors he had parodied, some of them more than once, and the authors he had not tackled yet, and he just shrugged his shoulders. "They're all yours, sweetie. I haven't the heart any more." I reminded him that in order for my efforts to reach an audience they would need to be posted up on his blog, which he had been more or less neglecting for a while now. "Sod the blog," he replied. When I pushed him on the matter, he gave me the password and told me I was welcome to post up whatever parodies I liked under his name. This I duly did, and it was in this way that I, in effect, became Gladwell the Parodist.

Then came the worst of it: the terrible week in which he got his stuff together and moved out of Milner's flat back to his own place. I didn't assist in the practicalities; it was well understood he had people to help him with those. I had my own role, however. Two evenings after the move he sat with me in our corner of the World's End and wept, and I felt so touched I actually put my arms around him.

"I can't do it," he sobbed. "I can't be alone like this, Antinous."

"It's Timothy," I replied. "My name's Timothy."

It was the rashness of a moment, and I never expected him to remember it.

He settled back into the single life remarkably quickly, so quickly that I was soon questioning how genuine his distress had been. It wasn't that he hadn't loved Aaron, or wasn't deeply wounded. I think now—now that I am able to look back and see him whole, so to speak—that Gladwell was always genuine in the instant. It was just that he changed so fast. Life and its riches sped by and he grabbed at whatever he could while he had the chance. Myself included.

Now that he was back in his house in Tufnell Park he began pressuring me to come over. He would squeeze my knee under the table and say, "What about it, then, Antinous? Shall we go back to mine?" Pouting, he would plead, "Surely you don't have to go home just yet?" When he found out where I lived he wheedled, "But that's perfect! My place is on your way." And when I steadfastly resisted he threatened to stop meeting me at the World's End any more.

I didn't take this seriously at first; I felt confident of his reliance on the special intimacy that had grown up between us. There were things about him only I knew, vulnerabilities I alone had witnessed. When anguish overcame him, it was to me that he must surely turn. Yet as the tumult of his separation from Milner receded I began to fear that he might not need me any longer, that I might even become associated with a time he wished to put firmly in the past. What if he were to lose interest? I would be swept away along with a hundred other passing fancies, he would move on to the next one and forget about me.

And then there was the matter of those novels of his. I wanted to read them so badly. I longed to see for myself if they were any good, whether Gladwell the artist had in fact had talent. Had he been right to give up on fiction and turn to parody? Were his bitterness and cynicism justified? If not, I felt in some obscure way, there might still be hope—hope for myself, that is, if not for him.

At last I could hold out no longer; there was only one thing for it. I brought the manuscript of my own unfinished novel to the World's End. He looked puzzled when I laid it on the table, and confused when I reminded him what it was, and of our bargain, which he seemed entirely to have forgotten. He picked it up and riffled the page corners, as if trying to count up how many tedious pages he would have to plough through.

"Oh, but... And is this *it*, Antinous? Well, my dear! Thank you. This is very kind."

"I'm not meaning to be kind. You insisted, remember. I show you mine and you show me yours."

He tittered like a schoolboy. "Oh, Antinous—promises, promises!" Then he gave a theatrical start. "But that gives me a wonderful idea." And he clutched the manuscript to his chest and looked at me wide-eyed.

"No... No..."

"Yes, yes! You come back to my place and I show you—mine!" And he threw his head back and laughed like a hyena.

"Your novels, you mean?"

"My novels—yes, of course I mean my novels!" But he only laughed the more.

"Why can't you bring them here?"

"No, no, darling. I couldn't possibly do that."

I argued, haggled, prevaricated. But it was no use. My fears and desires won out over my inner warnings. And that was how I ended up going to Tufnell Park.

— XIX —

THE QUESTIONING TOOK PLACE in a bright, windowless room of the police headquarters, a room in which there were no shadows and nowhere to hide.

I sat on one side of the table and Detective Liddington on the other. A female officer bore witness to our exchanges. On the table between us lay a recording device.

"This is completely ridiculous. Why on earth would I murder Ralph Gladwell? I barely knew the man."

"Yet you seem to have taken a great deal of interest in Mr Gladwell since his death."

"He was a great satirist. His death was a tragedy."

"To the extent that you have gone around interviewing his close family and friends, obtaining access to them under false pretences."

"Not under false pretences. I've been planning to write a short book about his work."

"What do you do for a living, Mr Nesbitt?"

"I'm an officer for the Arts Council."

"Yet you told Anwar Mussa"—he consulted a set of notes—"that you were writing a doctorate for Oxford University."

"I had to give myself some credibility. It isn't a crime, is it?"

"We'll come to the crime. You seem to have been very interested in certain unpublished manuscripts belonging to Mr Gladwell."

"His early novels, yes. I think they're important."

"Important?"

"For an understanding of Ralph's development as a writer. Couldn't I at least see them, Officer? To have them in my hands at last, and then have them snatched away—"

"You say you weren't a personal friend of Mr Gladwell's. Yet you call him Ralph."

"Well, yes. You can come to feel you know someone personally through their work."

"Can you, indeed. Then, there was no private correspondence between yourself and the victim?"

"The victim?"

"Mr Gladwell is the victim here." He looked at me strangely, then exchanged glances with his female sidekick.

"Yes, yes," I murmured. "I suppose he is."

"No private correspondence," the policeman repeated.

"None to speak of."

"Please speak of it."

"Just that I would occasionally comment on his blog. I dropped him the odd email. It doesn't really count."

"I see. Under what name would you comment?"

"I don't remember. My own, probably."

"Probably not, Mr Nesbitt."

I looked questioningly at him.

"There is no Timothy Nesbitt listed among the contributors to Mr Gladwell's blog."

"Oh—well... It's a long time since I posted anything."

"How long have you been following the blog?"

"About five years."

"That shows remarkable persistence."

"I'd prefer to call it loyalty. I loved reading it. It made me laugh."

"And in all this time you were never interested in meeting Mr Gladwell in person?"

"Not really. Why should I be?"

"A writer you admired. Who made you laugh."

"I didn't need to meet him. I don't need to meet any of the writers I admire. I can meet them through their work."

"Tell me—did you know that Mr Gladwell was gay?"

"That didn't interest me."

"I asked whether you knew about it."

"Yes, I knew. Everybody knew."

"How did you know? How did you know that everybody knew?"

"The internet is full of gossip."

"Then, you were following the online gossip about Mr Gladwell?"

"I… I don't know. I suppose I picked up on it."

"But online gossip about someone who, let's face it, was not exactly a celebrity—you'd have to go out of your way to pick that up. Wouldn't you?"

"I suppose so," I muttered.

Inspector Liddington stared at me severely. He made a note. "Then you *were* interested in Mr Gladwell personally, beyond the limits of his literary activities?"

"I admired him," I repeated, sullenly.

The Inspector consulted his notes. "You told Mrs Gladwell that you and her son collaborated together."

"From time to time. I don't know that we actually *collaborated*."

"Explain what you did do, then."

"I sent him some parodies I'd written. He adapted them for his blog."

"Then, you did enter into a private correspondence?"

"I'm not sure I'd call it a correspondence. I sent the stuff, he used it. That's all."

"That's all? Without so much as a by your leave, he took your work and plagiarised it for his blog?"

I laughed, but my laughter sounded strange in my own ears. "Parody is already a form of plagiarism. It hardly mattered."

"I see. Yet you chose to regard it as collaboration."

"I chose to call it that. To impress Mrs Gladwell. To get her to talk to me."

He tapped his pen on the desk. The sound was intensely irritating, but I kept my calm exterior. Inside, I was a roiling sea of fear. If they'd decided I had done it, they would push me, prod me, corner me until there was no way out. They were clever enough.

Inspector Liddington said, "What can you tell me about a girl called Julie Smith?"

"Nothing much."

"Come, come, Mr. Nesbitt. We both know better than that."

I didn't reply.

"Shall I tweak your memory for you? It was five years ago."

"I liked her, she didn't like me. She rejected me. End of story."

"Not quite. You then harrassed her," he consulted his notes, "for a period of nine months."

"I didn't harrass her."

"You stalked her, harrassed her and made her life a misery for nine months, until you were slapped with a restraining order. Didn't you then see a psychiatrist?"

"I don't see what this has to do with anything."

"Do you not?" Inspector Liddington stared at me for a few moments. Then he resumed his attack. "Who is Jim Tate?"

"Jim Tate?" I repeated.

"Yes. Jim Tate. Do you know anybody by that name?"

"Well, I'm Jim Tate. Everybody" (I gestured towards his notes) "will have told you that."

"You're Jim Tate?"

"Yes."

"There's no other Jim Tate that you're aware of?"

"No."

"Then who is Timothy Nesbitt?"

I cleared my throat. "I'm Timothy Nesbitt."

"You're Timothy Nesbitt." He turned his pen, over and over and over. "And what is the difference between Jim Tate and Timothy Nesbitt?"

"How do you mean?"

"How would you describe Jim Tate as distinct from Timothy Nesbitt?"

"I don't understand you."

"Well, these are two separate personalities with two different names. Maybe Jim is more confident and self-assured, while Timothy is—" he glanced at my hands, which were closed into fists just then, the knuckles white—"nervous and introverted. Maybe Jim is handsome, while Timothy is balding and a bit overweight. You get my drift?"

"I get your drift," I said, acidly. "It isn't about that."

"It isn't about what?"

"I'm not a nutter," I said. "I'm not schizophrenic."

"I'm glad to hear it. Why don't you tell me, then, why you used the alias Jim Tate, not only with Mr

Gladwell's friends and family but in all your online correspondence with him?"

A jolt passed through me. Our eyes met. He's bluffing, I told myself. He doesn't know half as much as he is implying. "Everyone uses aliases online."

"Not everyone. Mr Gladwell himself didn't."

"He didn't need to."

"No, he didn't need to. Because his private and public selves were at peace with each other."

"You could say that."

"But yours weren't."

"I didn't—"

"Yours weren't, because your private self was so lacking in confidence, so eaten up with rage and jealousy and self-hatred you couldn't go out in public without adopting a mask of some kind, a mask called Jim Tate. Isn't that the case?"

"No. It wasn't like that."

"And from behind that mask you were able to operate, to gain the trust of Mr Gladwell, to insinuate yourself into his life, to close in, and eventually to strike—"

"I didn't do that!" I shouted. "I didn't kill him!"

Inspector Liddington sat back and relaxed. Having got the violent reaction he wanted, he was satisfied, at least for the moment. He still had an ace or two up his sleeve, however. Removing an object from his pocket, he placed it upon the table.

"Do you recognise this?"

I sat looking at it with a sense of weariness. "It's a cigarette lighter."

"Belonging to whom?"

"Ralph gave it to Aaron Milner as a wedding present. When they split up Milner returned it."

"Correct. For someone who takes no interest in writers' personal lives you seem to know a lot of intimate details about Ralph Gladwell's."

I didn't reply.

"You gave this cigarette lighter to Aaron Milner. Can you tell me how you came to be in possession of it?"

"I told him that. Gladwell left it behind in the pub one evening. I picked it up."

"That pub would be the Duke of Wellington?"

"Yes."

"A place where Ralph Gladwell and his friends met regularly."

"I believe so, yes."

"You believe so. You believe so? Ralph Gladwell and his friends met regularly in the Duke of Wellington on a Wednesday evening for upwards of five years, and you *believe* so?"

"I know so, then."

"You knew they met regularly. Did you ever attend those meetings?"

"Not as such. I sat a bit off to the side."

"You mean you eavesdropped?"

"You'll be telling me that's a crime next."

"You sat off to the side without making yourself known, and listened in to their conversations."

"I meant to introduce myself. I didn't have the confidence."

"Although, in your own words, you *weren't really interested* in meeting Mr Gladwell in person?"

"That was before. Later on I was."

"I see. Later on you were." He and his colleague exchanged glances again. "And when they left at the end of the evening, you saw the lighter sitting on the table?"

"Yes."

"Why didn't you go straight after them and return it there and then?"

"It was already too late. They'd been gone too long."

"Are you sure about that?"

"Quite sure."

"And you didn't take any subsequent opportunity—the following week, for example, or the week after that?"

"I ... don't think I went there again."

"How convenient." He paused. "Can you explain why Mr Gladwell would even have brought the lighter to the pub, since he didn't smoke?"

"No, I can't. Should I be able to?"

He stared into my face. I stared back. He was headed down a blind alley with this one, and he knew it. He sighed, rustled his notes, and started on yet another tack. "What does the address 75, Hugo Road mean to you?"

I screwed up my face, thought about it, shook my head. "Should it mean something?"

"You don't recognise it? You have never visited that address?"

"Not so far as I can remember."

"You are not aware that it is Mr Gladwell's home address?"

"No."

"And you have never visited?"

"No."

"Perhaps you could explain to me, then," and he began laying in front of me various technical sheets, displaying images and data I could not possibly begin to understand, "why fingerprints matching yours were found at the address in question, which was also the scene of Ralph Gladwell's murder?"

A lump rose to my throat. I swallowed hard. "I have no idea."

"I'm sorry, Mr Nesbitt. Could you repeat that?"

"Where did you…" I began to sort through the sheets with trembling fingers. "This is a set-up of some kind. It has to be. Where did you get my fingerprints? These aren't my fingerprints."

"You say so, Mr Nesbitt. And yet your flat is simply covered in those same fingerprints."

"My flat? What do you mean?"

"I mean that during your absence at your parents' house in—Bognor Regis, isn't it?—we exercised a warrant and obtained entry to your flat. Where, I may add, we discovered a considerable amount of incriminating evidence."

Suddenly I couldn't get my breath. "This is outrageous. This is completely outrageous."

"I think you'll find it is perfectly in order and above board."

"You've set this whole thing up." I realised it with horror; my blood ran cold. "You're framing me."

"Hardly. Any trouble you find yourself in is entirely of your own making. We just played the cards you dealt us. You left London of your own accord. Didn't you? If you'd been at home when we called it would have made no difference. The only subterfuge was that of Mrs Gladwell, when she so obligingly brought you to High Wycombe. Otherwise, who knows," he chuckled slightly, "you might have been in Zanzibar by now."

"Then she never knew about the manuscripts," I whispered.

Inspector Liddington shrugged. "That's neither here nor there." He pushed back his chair, rose to his feet and leaned towards me, his hands on the table. "Let me repeat my question: Have you ever visited Ralph Gladwell's home address?"

Slowly, deliberately, I raised my eyes to his. "I was never there in my life," I answered.

He breathed out sharply through his nose, and for the first time I glimpsed the possibility of his becoming violent. It frightened me. He had a thick, rugby player's neck. His arms and hands were powerful.

He turned his back on me and walked away a few paces, circled that half of the room and then returned. The policewoman remained impassive, but a sudden sharp, sweaty smell suggested that she too was alarmed. Or perhaps it was just me.

Inspector Liddington remained standing and regarded me stonily as he inquired, "Can you describe your whereabouts between eight p.m. and midnight on the evening of the thirtieth of June?"

"I don't know. I don't keep a mental diary of all my movements. What day of the week was it?"

"It was a Tuesday, as I'm sure you're aware."

"Then I expect I came home from work, had dinner and went to bed."

"Is there anybody who could corroborate your account?"

"What—that I came home, had dinner and went to bed? Not really. It must make it so much easier for you," I added sarcastically.

But he was no longer interested in my protestations. "I put it to you," he said, "that on the evening of Tuesday the thirtieth of June you didn't go straight home from work at all."

"No?"

"No. On the contrary, you met with Ralph Gladwell on that evening at his home at 75 Hugo Road. While there, you and Mr Gladwell shared a bottle of red wine. You then had sex. At some point in the aftermath of your sexual encounter you quarreled and while Mr Gladwell was seated at his desk, helpless and unarmed, you stabbed him in the back seven times with this letter opener." The policewoman passed him an item in a clear plastic bag, he placed it on the table in front of me and examined my face carefully as I looked at it. I felt myself blench. "What did you quarrel about, Mr Nesbitt?"

"We didn't quarrel," I murmured.

"But you were at his house? You don't persist in denying that?"

"I don't..." Sweat had broken out all over my body. I gazed at the blade, the little blunt blade with its pearl handle. "I don't know... What's the point in denying it? You've already put my fingerprints all over the place. I don't stand a chance."

"Why on earth would we do that, Mr Nesbitt?"

"I don't know. Because you need a culprit. To make you look good. I'm an easy target."

He tutted at me patronisingly. "Really, now, Timothy. I think you need to come up with something better than that."

I started to cry.

"Sergeant Beddoes, would you fetch Mr Nesbitt a drink of water?" He sat down. A paper cup of water was handed to me. I swallowed it thirstily.

"Let's go back to that evening," the Inspector resumed. "You say you didn't quarrel. Why don't you tell me, in your own words, what did happen?"

"I don't remember."

"Take your time."

"I don't remember. I went home. I had dinner. I went to bed."

"Before that, then. On your way home. You stopped off at Tufnell Park tube station, didn't you? You went to Ralph Gladwell's house."

I rubbed my hand across my forehead, back and forth. I was trapped in a nightmare. Mrs Gladwell hadn't known about the manuscripts. If she hadn't lured me back, if she hadn't needed to stall me while she fetched the police, I would never have found them. My mind circled and circled around this conundrum.

"Ralph invited you there, didn't he?" the Inspector continued in his probing, unctuous way.

"No."

"He invited you there for around eight o'clock. You walked from Tufnell Park tube station. It was a cloudy evening. You climbed the steps of number seventy-five. You rang the bell. Ralph answered the door and you went in. And then?"

"And then?"

"Then what happened?"

"Nothing happened!" I shouted. "Wine, sex—don't you hear how ridiculous it all sounds? *I don't drink!* And I don't—"

"Have sex?"

My face burst into flame. "I don't have sex with men!" I yelled. Or women. Or anyone, I heard the voice of Hal taunting me in my mind, and saw the vision of his leering mouth.

The Inspector sighed heavily. He removed the awful object from my sight, passed it back to the female officer and wearily, sadly, replaced it with something else. Exhibit C. I tried, his body language seemed to say. I didn't want it to have to come to this. But you pushed me into it. You have only yourself to blame.

It was a mobile phone.

"Tell me," he said, "do you happen to recognise this phone?"

"Should I?"

"Perhaps, perhaps not. It's Ralph Gladwell's phone."

I stared at it. Vaguely, out of the mist, something troubling began to come back to me.

Inspector Liddington pushed the phone gently back and forth between his fingertips. "Tell me," he said again, and I began to wish it was he who had been murdered, "does the name Antinous mean anything to you?"

I felt a sharp stabbing sensation underneath my heart.

"Mr Nesbitt. Did you hear my question? I'll repeat it for you. Who is Antinous?"

"Mr Nesbitt. Are you Antinous?"

It was then that I think I must have begun screaming.

— XX —

GLADWELL GOT ME TO his house under false pretences: I know that now. It's my settled belief that he never intended showing me his novels. He wanted me there, with him, behind closed doors. That was the whole of it, and he grabbed his opportunity.

It was a warm summer's evening and still fully light when we stepped over the threshold into the chequered hallway. I had been here before, of course, but Gladwell was not aware of that. I remembered the black-and-white floor tiles, which looked immaculate, as though they had been laid last week; the antique umbrella stand and occasional table were new to me. The sense that I had trespassed under false pretenses, and must now take care to conceal the fact, added to my sense of danger and vulnerability.

Gladwell ushered me into the large, comfortable living room, which was furnished almost exactly as on my previous visit. There were a couple of big sofas covered by Oriental rugs. There was a dark polished floor and a steel fireplace fronted by an antique screen embroidered with birds of paradise. A huge abstract painting in reds and purples hung on the opposite wall, and the room was rendered private by half-closed Venetian blinds over the bay window. It was all so familiar I could only respond with a vague murmur when he inquired eagerly whether I liked his house.

Gladwell invited me to sit down and, pulling apart a pair of sliding doors with a smooth effort of his powerful arms, revealed an inner dining room beyond which, I knew, lay a contemporary kitchen. He returned from there shortly with a mug of tea for me and a glass of chilled white wine for himself.

"Milk and—two sugars?" He laughed. "Oh, Antinous, you are a cough drop!"

He sat down beside me on the sofa, allowed me to take no more than a couple of sips and gently removing the mug from my hands, placed it next to his glass upon the nearby coffee table. He then began trying to kiss me. I pushed him away.

"I didn't come here for that," I said, ridiculously.

He looked surprised, but not in the least offended. He was all innocence. "What *did* you come here for?"

"You know very well what."

"I don't! Remind me."

"Your novels."

Slapping a palm to his forehead, he exclaimed, "My novels!" He looked about him. Where, in this spotless house, could they possibly be? Under the sofa, perhaps? There was only a stray cork. Inside this cabinet? It was full of drink. "They could be upstairs," he suggested, looking eagerly at me.

"Then go find them."

He pouted; I should have suspected, though I had not fully imagined, his capacity to be whimsical. He rose shortly and disappeared upstairs. I sat waiting with my hands folded. After a while I remembered my mug of tea, and drank it down. It was already lukewarm; he had added too much milk. Soon afterwards, Gladwell reappeared empty-handed.

"I don't know what I can have done with them."

His bafflement seemed genuine, but with him there was no way of knowing. I wished now that I had risked accompanying him upstairs, to see how thoroughly he had conducted his search.

"I'll keep looking," he promised. "I might have left them at Aaron's, though. In which case, I'm afraid we're both out of luck." I reached for the plastic carrier bag which held my own manuscript, but he grabbed it back. "Oh, no—I hold on to this," he insisted.

In this way I was obliged to leave my hostage behind, but at least I managed to escape with my honour intact.

I don't know how I got home. I have no memory of that journey. As soon as I entered my flat I began gulping down water as though I had run a marathon. That night I barely slept. I don't know what troubled me more: the fact that Gladwell now had my unfinished novel in his possession or that he had tried to seduce me. When I did drop off, towards dawn, my dreams were a tangle of humiliation. I woke, disturbingly, to the sound of my own protests.

I didn't hear from him again for several days. I sent him a couple of texts; they went unanswered. I carried on about my business, fuming. An intolerable pressure was building up inside me. All that had gone to make me what I was now seemed summed up in my present impasse. You laugh at me, I laugh at you, Gladwell had said. But I was the only one who was being laughed at.

It was a full two weeks before he finally called. He wanted to meet, not at the World's End, but at his house in Tufnell Park. He had found the novels, he told me. If I would come to his place at eight p.m. on the thirtieth he would hand them over.

I knew it would be pointless to prevaricate. Besides,

while one half of me was angry, resentful, and didn't want to go, the other half was drawn irresistibly by a sense of chosenness, even of privilege: for me, Gladwell had lost none of his glamour. To be asked to his house was to be invited behind the curtain and into the charmed circle. I could not have refused him, even if I believed that danger and degradation awaited me there.

The thirtieth of June was grey, overcast and coolish. I arrived at the house in Hugo Road a little after eight, still dressed in my work clothes because I had not seen the point in going home only to come out again. I'd worked as late as I could, finishing up various stupefying chores, and then dined at a Prêt à Manger close to the office. I had various questions I wanted to put to Gladwell—an interrogation, really—but they all flew out of my head the moment he answered the front door dressed in a silk paisley housecoat worthy of Noël Coward. On his tall, spare form it looked nothing other than distinguished. He greeted me warmly; he seemed genuinely delighted to see me. But I was disconcerted when instead of ushering me into the living room he led me straight upstairs to his study on the first floor.

This, on my clandestine tour, had been almost empty. It was now transformed. It was as cheerfully chaotic as the main reception area had been elegant and spare. This, in fact, was the setting for my dreams, with its floor-to-ceiling bookcases packed with books stuffed in every which-way, its overflowing desk and its shabby sofa strewn with colourful throws. There was a very deep, threadbare armchair filled with heaps of what looked like student essays, of which the lower layers, like sedimentary rocks, appeared to have festered there for quite some time. On the mantel above the fireplace were several half-burnt candles, suggesting bohemian and romantic evenings, and over the whole room hung an air of sensuality, of human odour mixed with perfume and desire.

Yet the room was inviting, cosy, warm behind its closed red curtains which shut out the grey unseasonal evening. This, I sensed, was Gladwell's true domain, the room in which he worked and wrote. Here he was—or had been—Gladwell the Parodist: the man I had first admired, whom I had sought to impress and finally to know.

Ralph seemed to appreciate my sense of awe at being admitted to his inner sanctum. Smiling, he spread his arms and announced, "Welcome to my kingdom. Welcome, Antinous!"

I sat down on the ancient sofa, which sank beneath my weight. My host, clearly prepared for this entire scenario, brought forward a bottle of red wine and two glasses. He began casually to unscrew the top.

"You know I don't drink wine."

"Nonsense. You can't refuse this. It's hardly even alcohol. It's chilled Beaujolais." He proceeded to pour us each a full glass. I set mine down on an old ship's chest which stood close by.

"What about your novels?" I said.

"All in good time, sweetie, all in good time." He sat down beside me; when the flaps of his housecoat opened I received the distinct impression that he was wearing nothing underneath. He picked up my glass and placed it once more in my hand. "I want you to taste this and tell me it isn't truly delightful. A toast." He clinked his glass against mine. "To literature."

He drank. I followed suit. The chilled wine was not unpleasant. It was rather good, in fact. Gladwell, who was closely watching my reaction, smiled. "You see. I told you you would like it. A chilled Beaujolais never did anyone any harm. Now then," crossing his legs, he snuggled closer, "isn't this more cosy? We can do and say what we like here. It's just the two of us."

I was more than aware of that; my heart was thumping. I took a big swallow of wine without really intending to.

"Antinous," he breathed, and brushed the back of his hand lightly across my cheek. I shuddered. I hardly knew whether what I was feeling should be classified as desire or disgust. Suddenly he set down his glass, bounced away from me and headed over to the desk. "I almost forgot! Your novel." Bringing the manuscript back with him to the sofa, he crossed his legs once more, revealing bare flesh all the way up to the thigh. He began leafing through the pages. "You know, you're really very talented. You ought to finish this."

I smiled sceptically. "You don't mean it."

"Of course I do. You must finish and publish it. Only, when you do so, promise me it will be under the name of 'Antinous.'"

Was he laughing at me? He must be. Yet my desire to be taken seriously was so desperate, I could have cried. "Oh, I don't know... I mean, if I were even to..." But I broke off because, letting the manuscript slip from his fingers and fan out onto the floor, he leaned across and brought his face within inches of my own. I could feel his breath on my cheeks; it smelt of wine. He began running his hand firmly up and down my leg, bringing it almost as far as my crotch and then away again, so that I started to feel as though my teeth would chatter.

Suddenly he laughed. "Why are you wearing all these silly clothes?"

I looked down at my black trousers and longsleeved shirt, in which I had baked in my airless office all day long. "I've just come from work," I explained, though he wasn't in the least interested.

"Let me undo these, at least." And he began unfastening the buttons on my shirt from collar to navel.

I remained impassive, helpless as a fly in a spider's web. The small amount of wine I had drunk had gone straight to my head, not surprisingly, since I had no resistance to alcohol. I felt as though I were floating. I could hardly believe what was happening to me.

Gladwell began running the palm of his hand all over my exposed torso. I lay there tingling. When he bent down and applied his tongue to my nipples I caught my breath. His response was in one swift movement to pull the shirt from my back. I heard the seams crack as he tore it from me and threw it onto the floor. He began licking me all over my chest in an almost frantic way.

I reached over for my glass and took several more gulps of wine. *He* may not have needed to be drunk but *I* certainly did; needless to say, I had never done anything like this before. Within seconds my head was swirling and I was being swept down a fast river of sensual imperative. There seemed no way of resisting the forces which had overtaken me.

Gladwell, having dispensed with the top half of my clothing, began unfastening the button on my trousers and pulling down the zip. Practised as he clearly was in these operations, it was not easy, and I wriggled about in an effort to assist him. Even in my half-sedated state I was uncomfortably aware of my own physical shortcomings and the flabbiness of my waistline. We managed together to ease me out of my trousers and they too landed somewhere on the floor. I was now down to my underwear: a sense of how vulnerable and without dignity I was flashed through my mind for an instant, but I pushed it away, convinced that Ralph could not be doing this to me unless he were to be trusted.

The things he was now doing with his tongue, lips and hands were bringing me to the brink of total self-abandonment. I was amazed to hear my own involuntary sighs and moans. All of a sudden he got up, lunged over to a pair of double doors and swept them apart with a single powerful action, revealing the bedroom beyond with its king-size bed. Study and bedroom were designed on the same principle as the rooms below, but the effect here was dramatic, almost explosive: the doors parting on his true theatre of passion.

Urging me to my feet, he pulled me over to the bed, repeating in a mesmeric murmur, "Antinous, Antinous, come on Antinous." I was hardly in a condition to resist. I stumbled across and fell, together with him, onto the crimson satin counterpane scattered with cushions. Here was a man who took his bedroom very seriously. Out of my whirling reverie I caught sight of erotic pictures, draperies, lit candles and, hanging directly above the bed, an enormous Venetian chandelier. I may have worked in the arts, but no-one I had ever met embraced high camp the way that Gladwell did.

He now flung off his own clothes without waiting for assistance, revealing his long, lean body with its surprisingly muscular torso. It was not, clearly, the body of a young man, but it was wiry and well-kept, its loose, weathered skin strangely attractive to me: the body of a man well-travelled and still adventurous. The scanty hair around his scrotum and large, erect penis was entirely grey, something I found peculiarly exciting, although a residual nervousness prevented me from taking any initiative. Probably noticing this, he maintained his assertive role and continued stimulating my supine form. His tongue was like a snake's: he kept giving my belly and then my penis little flickering licks, then suddenly swallowed it whole, nearly driving me wild with suspended pleasure.

He did not deliver on his seeming promises, however, but when I was at my most desperate abandoned me with an almost callous movement which was in itself tantalising. Next thing I knew he had mounted me from behind and forced his way in with one brutal thrust. I cried out in pain. He was merciless, persisting in his object without reprieve, continuing his thrusts while keeping one arm tightly clamped around my chest as with his other hand he gripped my penis. As his rhythmic movements quickened into frenzy I screamed in mingled agony and bliss.

The violence and fury of this moment seemed to me to extend indefinitely. We had become a machine of flesh, perfectly and implacably conjoined, shrieking its way to inevitable climax. And that arrived like a miracle, synchronised, as we both groaned out our pleasure. Then the machine fell apart: we disengaged and collapsed onto the bed, panting.

"Now, Antinous, you've been well and truly fucked!"

Didn't I know it. As soon as the instant of orgasm had passed, the more persistent and less pleasant one of pain asserted itself. My back passage was on fire; when I put my fingers there I brought them away bloody. I was suddenly outraged. "Look what you've done to me! I'm bleeding. Do you see that?"

He rolled over and sat up, smiling. "Don't worry about that, you'll soon get over it."

"What do you mean? Did it ever occur to you that this has never happened to me before?"

"That was all too evident, my sweet."

"And so you just forced yourself—just bludgeoned your way in—"

"It might not be the best way, but it is my way. What did you expect—that I would ask permission?"

I couldn't reply; I felt raped. I was livid.

"Come on, Antinous. Don't be moody. You enjoyed it, didn't you?" Quite lovingly, Gladwell put his arm around me, but I threw him off. I couldn't deny that I had enjoyed it, nor that I despised myself for having done so. "I'm sorry," he continued. "I truly am. You know I wouldn't hurt you for the world. But believe me, this will pale into insignificance next to all the other times. You've lost your virginity, that's all. Be glad of it."

What was the man talking about? The man—the monster! I wanted to rip his heart out.

"Come on, I'll take you to the bathroom. We'll get you cleaned up and sorted out in no time."

"I'll see to myself, thank you!" I got up off the bed. Every movement was agony. Shuffling out onto the landing I found the bathroom under my own steam and without much difficulty. It was a black-and-white affair with an old-fashioned suite and big chrome taps. There was a thick white rug on the tiled floor and I derived some satisfaction from allowing my blood to spatter onto it.

I sat on the edge of the bath with the door locked and ran the cold tap, applying soothing splashes to my rear end as I watched, with considerable self-pity, the pink-tinged water run away down the plughole. As I did so I wondered how on earth I had found myself in this humiliating situation. I had to admit that I was largely responsible. I had been under no illusions as to Gladwell's man-eating proclivities, yet I had walked into his trap with my eyes wide open. I had been flattered by his attentions, there was no doubt about it. He had made me feel important to myself, and heaven knows there was little else in my life to feel important for. Over the months and years he had become my mirror; I had modelled myself after him even as he had stepped down off his pedestal and handed on the torch. And there, indeed, was the nub of the matter. He had taunted me, minutes before, with having been well and truly fucked. If that was the case, then I might retort that he had fucked himself.

There came a knocking at the bathroom door. "Antinous? Are you all right? What are you up to in there?" He rattled the handle. "Why have you locked it? For goodness' sake, let me in." I sat there silently, letting him stew for a while, then languidly dried myself off on one of his soft white towels, fastened it around my waist and without hurrying opened up the door. "Antinous, sweetie! I thought you might have done yourself a mischief. Are you all right?" I said I was fine, and stalked past him into the study to retrieve my clothes.

He followed, stark naked, continuing to plead. "Don't sulk, darling. Will you at least look at me? Must you get dressed so—so stompily? Oh, if you *will* insist—" He picked up his own dressing-gown from the floor and pulled it on, never for one moment ceasing his stream of talk.

"Honestly, it isn't the end of the world. I know what you're feeling, but truly—Look at me!" Having dressed, I allowed him to come close enough to turn my head with his hand. "Antinous, look at me!" I gazed stonily at him. "It was a beautiful thing that we did—a beautiful, glorious thing. Kiss and make up!" He kissed my unresponsive lips. "Forgive me, Antinous!"

"My name isn't Antinous."

"Timmy, then."

Icily I said, "Only my mother calls me Timmy."

"Oh, dear. How to placate you? I'll make you some tea. Tea is what you like, isn't it? I'll make you some camomile. It's very soothing."

I didn't say no, and he began fiddling around with a kettle in the corner of the study. My anger was dissipating, or I thought it was. I tried to sit down; a sharp pain jabbed through me and I jumped up again. "I can't even sit down!" I exclaimed bitterly.

"I'm so sorry, An—Tim—Jim. I can't say sorry enough. Honestly, I'd forgotten you were a virgin."

"I do wish you'd stop using that word."

"Why? It's a beautiful word. I love that I was your first. We'll always have that, won't we, An—Jim. Oh, do let me call you Antinous."

He handed me the tea. I drank it down; I was completely sober.

"Are you ever going to forgive me?" he insisted.

"It depends." The tea *was* soothing. I found myself beginning to think more clearly. "Where are those novels of yours?"

"Oh, really. You're not going to hold me to that, are you?" When he screwed up his face he looked, in my eyes at least, quite ugly. "They're not at all interesting, I can assure you."

"Why don't you let me be the judge of that?"

"They're really the most embarrassing juvenilia. I should have burnt them years ago."

"All the more reason why you should let me see them."

"They're virgin work. The novels of a virgin—just like yours!" He let out an ugly laugh. I felt my blood flame.

"Are you laughing at me?"

"Oh, Antinous, Antinous! What are we if we cannot laugh at ourselves?" Once more he tried to approach me; I jerked away. "All that stuff—why don't we put it behind us? All that tedious stuff."

"What stuff?"

"Literature—writing—all that crap! I'm sick to death of it."

A puff of harsh laughter escaped me. "It's the only thing we have in common!"

Gladwell looked hurt. "You don't mean that. All right—not literature. I still care for that, of course. In fact, that's precisely my point. The whole evil rigmarole, the writing, the failure, the jealousy—I'm sick and tired of it. It's been coming on me for months; you must have noticed. I tell you, Antinous, I don't want to do it any more. I don't want to tear people down. I want to live and let live. And realising that has made me feel so free, so light. It's quite wonderful." He did, in fact, seem genuinely happy and relieved. "It's like pulling myself out of the mire of a bad relationship. I feel reborn." His face was radiant.

"What are you saying?"

"No more parody! I'm on the wagon."

I stared at him in disbelief. "You can't mean that."

"I absolutely do. I forsake cruelty. And in proof of it, I'll show you what I'm going to do." He leapt behind his desk and began firing up the computer.

I carefully set down my mug. Bit by bit, the meaning of his words began to penetrate my idiot's brain. He meant that at the vital pass, at this moment of crisis, having fucked me over, he was going to proceed to fuck me over, to abandon the attitude that had shaped my life. That having spoiled my chances with his own bitterness, his cynicism, his destructiveness, his hilarious, mordant humour, he was now ready to forswear it all.

"You can't be serious," I said.

"I am about this. It's the dawn of a new era." He started tapping away on the keyboard, hooking up to the internet.

"You have to be joking. Do you have any idea what you've done to me and my life? You *made* me. I wouldn't be what I am if it weren't for you."

"Really, Antinous?" He turned and looked at me with his mouth half-open. "That's extraordinary."

"You fucking *destroyed* me. I might have made something of myself if it weren't for you."

"I've no idea what you're talking about." He turned back to the computer and went on typing.

"I might have finished that novel. Now I never shall. What are you doing?"

"I'm going to kill Gladwell the Parodist!"

The blood drained from my heart. Gladwell was logging in to his blog account, using the password he had only recently supplied me with. I saw then what he planned to do. He was going to shut down the blog and delete the archives. He was gaily going about the erasure of our mutual life.

"You utter bastard," I said.

Gladwell seemed unconcerned. He was busy at the keyboard. In an access of fury I grabbed the first weapon that came to hand. It was a pearl-handled letter-opener which lay somewhat incongruously on the desk among the technological trappings of the twenty-first century. Seizing it in my fist I brought it down with all my power onto the back of my nemesis. He seemed no more than surprised at first, as if something had fallen on him by accident. Then he turned to look at me, and the expression in his eyes was almost grateful. The blade, though slight, emerged from the impact undamaged. Gladwell groaned. Possessed by a red rage I thrust it into him again and again, feeling at the same time a sort of exultation of hatred. It passed through the thin fabric of his housecoat and into his flesh with the ease of a fruit knife paring up an apple. There was surprisingly little blood. Gladwell collapsed face down onto the desk with his head on the keyboard. For the final few thrusts his upper body lolled unresponsively and I knew he must be dead, but was unable to stop myself. The catharsis was tremendous.

It was over. I dropped the knife onto the desk with a clatter, only to pick it up again and wipe it off on the tail of my shirt. I then placed it back on the desk; I had no idea why. I proceeded to act haphazardly. I had a vague notion about fingerprints, but conscious that I couldn't possibly conduct a thorough job (there was no way I could remember everything I had touched since entering) I only wiped things down half-heartedly here and there. Since I didn't really exist, certainly not as a figure in Gladwell's life, and had no police record, I didn't see what use my fingerprints could be. There was always our online correspondence, of course. I had no concept how to dispose of this, other than a most brutal and straightforward one: I pulled the plug of the computer from its socket, grabbed the nearest heavy object—it was a bronze figurine of a naked man, I think—and smashed it up. The violence of this frightened me more than what I had previously done. I began trembling. Then I realised I should have looked for his novels on the computer before smashing it.

The novels... The novels. Where in this morass might they be? I checked through the pile of essays on the armchair. I searched through the drawers of the desk. I opened up the cupboards under the bookcases and began throwing out their contents, which landed in untidy heaps on the floor. Panic seized me for the first time as I began to realise how long it would take to hunt through all this material. I drew several deep breaths in an effort to calm myself. I began leafing methodically through the documents.

In all this time, Gladwell himself remained still, though something within me refused to believe that he was really dead. I avoided looking at him. He lay at the desk as though sleeping. I persuaded myself that he was actually asleep. The actions I had so recently performed had already assumed the nature of a dream.

At one point I stumbled across some pages of typescript that seemed familiar. It dawned on me that they came from my own novel, which still lay fanned out on the floor where Gladwell had dropped them earlier. This was, most assuredly, incriminating evidence. I collected them up and put them in a plastic bag.

The room was now a bombsite: books were pulled from the shelves, cupboards and drawers lay open, there were papers everywhere. I looked at the clock on the mantelpiece. It was nearly midnight. If I wanted to catch the last tube I must be on my way. I panicked again as I looked to the bedroom. The bed was still in its rumpled state. My semen was on the sheets. I went through and pulled the sheets from the bed onto the floor; I had no idea why. In the act of doing so I found Gladwell's phone on the bedside cabinet. It was switched off. I took and placed it in the plastic bag.

I felt reasonably certain that the novels were not here. I got my things together and went downstairs. On my way to the front door I put my head into the living room. It was clean and tidy, as before, and eerily quiet. I wanted to look in there for the manuscripts, but there wasn't time. I had a strong intuition that they wouldn't be there, though. Then I noticed the lighter standing on the mantelpiece. I suppose Gladwell had been using it to light the fire. I walked over and picked it up. It was much heavier than I'd expected. I felt a sudden fierce desire to have it, so I dropped that, too, into the plastic bag.

I left the lights on exactly as they had been when I arrived and pulled the front door to behind me. It was dark outside. I was still in so much pain I could barely walk.

I caught the last tube and reached home around twelve thirty.

— XXI —

I pleaded guilty. And, quite frankly, confessing was a relief. Part of me wanted more than anything to get caught, come clean, be punished, have it over with.

I don't think anyone really understood why I killed him, and I didn't expect them to. They seemed to think I must have been out of my mind. On the contrary, I was more clear-headed at that moment than I have been, probably, at any time in my life. He got what he deserved. What's more—as I've come to realise—he got what he wanted.

Nevertheless, they decided I was bonkers. Which means I probably won't see freedom again this side of eternity, and will spend the rest of my life mixing with the criminally insane. But what is freedom, anyway? I'm not convinced I ever had it in the first place. If I did, I certainly didn't make much use of it.

My mother was the most upset of anyone. I suppose my greatest regret is for what this has done to her. When she came to visit, I begged her repeatedly to try and get hold of his manuscripts. She's a normal, kindly person; I thought if anyone could manage it, she could. But all she would do was cry, so I gave up asking.

I tried my lawyer too, but she doesn't understand anything.

Why was I so hell-bent on having the novels? That was what everybody wanted to know. As if it were even relevant to the case. I didn't kill Gladwell for the novels. I killed him because it was just and necessary, and because, of course, I was very, very angry. My one mistake was killing him before laying hands on his manuscripts.

The court and Gladwell's friends and the newspapers were all wide of the mark. I didn't kill Gladwell out of revenge. I killed him as an act of self-defence. Parodying his fiction would have been my revenge. I needed to do it like scratching a permanent itch. No writer in history ever deserved it more. Then I would have exposed him on his own blog.

First I would post his novel. Then I would post my parody of it. The great satirist, the scoffer, the debunker of high seriousness, would have his own high seriousness debunked. And I, whose aspirations had been done to death by his laughter, would have the last laugh. The sweetness of that. The delight. A work of art: the Parodist himself torn limb from limb.

It was a consummation worth getting caught for.

That's my whole confession. Now I'm done with writing. There's still plenty to read, of course. A whole library full of trash I could have such fun with. But as time passes I feel less and less the urge to make fun of literature, whether high or low. I only wish I could take pleasure from a single page of it.

Of course, in a way, I do feel sorry for Gladwell. He was once my hero, after all. And I see in the course of his life a sad tale of failure: hopeful, angry, sardonic, mournful, dead. The dead always earn our pity to some degree, which is why, while I live, I am still deemed undeserving.

Everyone wanted to know who killed Gladwell the Parodist. And now they do. But who killed whom? That is the real question.

About the author

Tamar Yellin is the author of three published works of fiction and many unpublished ones. She has been awarded the inaugural Sami Rohr Prize for Jewish literature, the Ribalow Prize and the Reform Judaism Prize. She was also shortlisted for the Jewish Quarterly/Wingate Prize and the Edge Hill Prize and longlisted for the Frank O'Connor International Short Story award. She lives in Yorkshire, England.
@tamar_yellin
www.tamaryellin.com

Previous titles by Tamar Yellin:

The Genizah at the House of Shepher
Kafka in Brontëland and other stories
Tales of the Ten Lost Tribes

Lightning Source UK Ltd.
Milton Keynes UK
UKHW022244011122
411471UK00002B/21/J